KARMA WILL CLAP BACK

JACQUELINE GREENE

KARMA WILL CLAP BACK

God's Word will Stand Forever
and It Changes for None

JACQUELINE GREENE

Unless otherwise indicated, all Scripture quotations are taken from the King James Version of the Bible. Some direct quotations from scripture are in bold face type.

ISBN : 9780578759029

DEDICATION AND ACKNOWLEDGEMENTS

First, I give thanks and praises to my Lord and Savior Jesus Christ for inspiring me to write this book. I thank God for my husband and friend, Lagee Andre Greene, and for his constant love and support. Thank you for showing me the true meaning of marriage. Thanks be to God for my daughter Sheron and my grand-daughter Nya, you both make me so proud. Always remember that God's way is the only way and his Word changes for none.

I also thank God for all of those, too numerous to name, who have supported me with advice, encouragement and inspiration throughout the years. May the Lord bless, keep and reward you for taking your time to invest in me.

I pray that the words in this book will lead you to live a life well-pleasing to our Father. May we avoid all of the pitfalls the devil has placed in our pathway to destroy our marriages and to abort our destinies. I pray that you will obey the Word and arise to achieve all that God has for you. Remember that it is your Father's good pleasure to give you His Kingdom.

Jacqueline Greene

Table of Contents

Chapter- 1 1

Chapter- 2 9

Chapter- 3 15

Chapter- 4 18

Chapter- 5 23

Chapter- 6 27

Chapter- 7 29

Chapter- 8 35

Chapter- 9 38

Chapter- 10 41

Chapter- 11 47

Chapter- 12 49

Chapter- 13 58

Chapter 14 63

Chapter- 15 70

Chapter- 16 75

Chapter- 17 80

Chapter- 18 89

Chapter- 19 97

Chapter- 20 102

Chapter- 21 110

Chapter- 22 115

Chapter- 23 120

CHAPTER- 1

You see life has a way of giving you back exactly what you feed it. Momma would always make me chuckle when she would say chile, you are sure to get what you pay for in this life. My mother Esther Freight was a hard-working island woman. She emigrated from the British Virgin Islands to the American owned Virgin Islands at the young age of 18. Her mom Edie died when my mother was a baby. My mother was raised by her father Sam and his wife Tessa. Momma was quick to say that she wasn't abused but she often felt more like an inconvenience.

I would always wonder why she chose the name Karma for me, was I her Karma? A girl must ponder these things, you know. I had no doubt that my mother loved me, but her life was not an easy one. She was always so quick to give so much of herself but received very little in return. I would like to think that she saw me as a blessing from God, her just reward and therefore her Karma. I did my best Momma, I really did my best.

Karma Will Clap Back

As you may have already figured out, my name is Karma and I have been giving for so long that I am certain that good things will return to me, right? Some would say my faith in the unknown is foolish but who really knows for sure. I got married at the tender age of twenty-three, what did I know? Children should be forbidden to marry until at least the age of 30. At least at that point, they would have some gained some insight and a bit of common sense, I think.

My husband's name is Will. Quite appropriate since I am still wondering when Will he love me? When Will he treat me better? What Will it take for me to leave him and the Will lives on. We have one beautiful 8-year old daughter together and her name is Faith. I did say we have one child together which implies that there are other children somewhere. I have been told that Will has one other child, but he has always denied it. One day I expect to receive a knock on the door and this famous child will emerge from darkness into the marvelous light. I wonder what Will he say then? Yes, Will Porter, what will you say then?

Today is my birthday. I have just reached the tender age of 36. Glory be to God. I am sitting in my living room, lights are dimmed, sipping some wine and reminiscing about my life. Don't judge me about the wine. A little wine can't hurt nobody, and Jesus did turn the water into wine at that wedding.

Where is Will, you ask? Honey, your guess is as good as mine. I have not seen my husband in two days. I hear you in the background saying maybe you should be worried, maybe something happened to him. I say to you, I used to worry, and I used to fret when he would disappear for days on end, and wouldn't answer his phone or respond to texts to let me know that he was alright. But then, he would just walk in the house as if nothing happened. Hey babe, anything to eat? I would find my blood boiling and I would want to kill him, smack him, poison him but I always remembered that Karma is a beast. So, I continue to stay quiet, hold my peace and let God fight this battle.

Yes, I said God. You see I got saved shortly after we were married and of course Will doesn't believe in the God thing. What is saved, you say? Saved is making an open declaration that you believe and accept that Jesus is the son of God and God raised him from the dead. I was about 25 when I accepted the Lord Jesus Christ as my Lord and Savior. I guess it was just fitting since I always believed in doing the right thing. I reasoned that if I am right about the God thing, then I get to go to heaven and if I am wrong, it is still okay since there's nothing wrong with living right and doing right in the first place. It is all a win-win situation in my mind anyway. But Will said I suffer from low self-esteem and the God thing is just my desire for everyone to love me. The psychologist in him has it all figured out but that is truly not the case.

I am five foot one and drop dead gorgeous. I have brown eyes, smooth chocolate skin, curves in all the right places and trust me, low self-esteem is not one of my issues. I can hang with the best of them. One of my problems is that I am married to a man who does not respect nor love me at this point in our relationship. I sit back and wonder where we went wrong. Surely if it takes two to make a thing go right, then it also takes two to make a thing go wrong. O Will, where did we go wrong?

I was so deep in thought that I didn't hear the door open. My husband staggered into the room and flopped down on the chair opposite me. Any food baby? What did I tell you?

Obviously, he had been out drinking. I looked over at my husband and felt hurt coupled with a whole lot of sadness. If we can't fix this relationship, what will happen to our daughter Faith? Will she be able to thrive despite the absence of her father? I hear you clearly saying, what makes you assume he will be absent and won't stay in his daughter's life. Now let us be real, how many brothers you know stick around when access to the well has dried up. Very few indeed and I know what my husband will and what he won't do. Trust me on this one, he won't be there.

I even think about my daughter now living in this unhealthy environment. What is this going to do to her in the long term? Is it better to stay with Will or just leave? These are some of the issues I find myself constantly grappling with lately. Am I doing an injustice to her, to me or even to him? Could I find love elsewhere? But I keep holding onto my faith, God will turn this situation around in only a matter of time, won't he? God are you listening, I am still waiting, after all it has only been eleven years. Yes, I did say, eleven years.

I have two cool friends, Darlene and Oprah. Those girls are my besties, I can tell them anything and not worry about it traveling down the road. In fact, they are the ones who led me to the Lord and showed me how great and merciful God truly is and how he loves us all. My besties and I grew up together, went to the same high school, same college. We have carried each other's secrets and burdens for a long time. Will calls us the Godly Girls. At least he says the name God when talking about us even if he doesn't really believe in Him. We are always praying for my husband and my marital relationship.

Darlene and Oprah are both married and seem to have loving marriages. They both got married in their thirties, so they are still in that honeymoon phase. The difference is that both of their husbands are saved and governed by a conscience and a belief in God. On the other hand, my husband is governed by his lower half and an absolute hatred for organized religion. He calls the pastors all sorts of terrible names, including poverty pimps, jokers, con artists and the list goes on. I pray every day for his deliverance. Lord, when will you answer me? It would be so easy to leave but I know the God that I serve. There is nothing too difficult for Him.

So many people give up just when their prayer request is about to be answered. Not me. I am going to hold on for dear life. I pray for God's wisdom and direction every day, especially since I don't want to be holding on to something that God has clearly told me to let go. God has not told me let Will go and to give up on my marriage, unlike countless others who have told me to run like a chicken with his head cut off.

But I am fighting this battle on my knees, yessiree, on my knees. Although my besties touch and agree with me in prayer, I often wonder if they feel as if I should flee too. They would never admit it, but I wouldn't blame them if they did. They love me and want only the best for me. Sometimes the pain can be so unbearable, like tonight, but I pray and keep it moving. How does a husband not acknowledge his wife's birthday?

When we first got married, every occasion was a celebration. We celebrated birthdays, anniversaries, promotions and any excuse we could find to have a party. Those were the good old days. Now I sit and drink my wine and reminisce about those glory years. I believe in marriage and all of the vows that I made before God. Some say that I can leave, and God will not hold me accountable since the Bible teaches us not to be unequally yoked. Some say I have a get out of jail card since I married my husband when we were both unbelievers. It would have been different if I had married him and I was a believer at the time, and he was not. In that instance, only his adultery would have set me free. I guess I am free to divorce but what would that say about my faith in God. I trust God completely and I am just waiting for him to work this situation here out. But Lord, can you speed this up, I am reminding you again that it has only been uh 11 years.

My husband again mutters, if there is any food to eat? This time with some annoyance in his voice. It is taking every fiber in my body to get up and go into the kitchen. As I get up, I start praying because I am not sure how this is going to turn out today. My period is about to come, and I am not feeling particularly godly at the moment. Hormones are flying and I am so pissed. Lord, please get these hormones under control or I am going to go upside this man's head. I hear that still small voice say, "Wait and be of good courage." I replied and said I am tired of waiting God. Then I heard the other one say, babe. You talking to me? Did you find anything for me to eat? It took all in me to answer, "not yet." I then opened up the refrigerator and put something together for my husband to eat. I placed it on the table and went to sleep. Not sure what time he came to bed, but as usual he kept to his side and I slept on my side. What a joke of a marriage. Good night ya'll.

CHAPTER- 2

I wake up to the sun beaming into my bedroom. I look over to see my husband sprawled out and snoring up a storm. How I learned to live with that snoring is beyond me. I remember when we first got married, I would spend half the night with a pillow over my head or laying on the bathroom floor trying to get some relief from the battle going on between his lungs, nose and throat. Unfortunately, the battle is still raging, and I have become their prisoner of war. Surprisingly, I have learned to adapt to the nose, I mean noise. This is what we call domestic abuse.

Anyway, as I was saying, I woke up to this beautiful sunny day. I get out of bed, say my prayers and head to Faith's room. She is also fast asleep. What time is it? I look at my watch and see that it is 5:30 a.m. What day is it again? Oh, Saturday. I quickly go over the things that I have to do today. Faith has dance practice at the church at 1 pm and I have choir practice. I need to go grocery shopping and I need to cook the meal for Sunday. Of course, I also have to clean up this place, it looks like a disaster zone.

All of a sudden, my telephone starts to ring. What in the world? Who would be calling my landline instead of my cellphone at this ungodly hour? Matter of fact, who would be calling so early in the morning period. It had better not be one of those annoying telemarketers. I look at the caller ID and see that it is Will's mother Hannah. Unlike most, I love my mother-in- law. She is truly an angel here on Earth. One of the reasons I put up with Will is that it would devastate his momma if I were to leave. She keeps telling me how devastated she would be, and I believe her. Who else could deal with his nonsense? Sometimes I wonder if part of the devastation would be that she would be the one having to deal with his nonsense.

I pick up the phone and immediately ask Momma Hannah, is everything alright? She was silent for a few moments and then she said that she is at the hospital with Will's brother Abraham and his wife Patsy (Sugar). She started to sniffle but managed to say that Abraham was just diagnosed with prostate cancer, Stage 4. I was floored. So many things started running through my mind. How could this be? Why don't men listen and go to the doctor? Sugar told me how long she has been trying to get him to go to see a doctor. Wow. How would Will handle this? He and Abraham were very close. They were 2 years apart. Abraham was the younger of the two and he simply idolized his older brother. His wife Sugar and I were not only church sisters, but we were both united in praying for our spouses.

Momma Hannah would always send up prayer for her boys. One thing I know, Momma Hannah is one praying woman. She would often say that Sugar and I were God's answer to her prayers. At this moment, I had to encourage her. I told her that God will perform a miracle and save her son. I reminded her that all things will work out for her good since we know that she loves the Lord. She told me she was at Salvation Hospital and I told her we would be there shortly. I called Darlene and asked her if she could come and get Faith and take her to her dance practice. She said she would need at least an hour. I went back into my bedroom and decided to get on with it. I woke up Will dreading his reaction since I know that he is definitely not a morning person.

Of course, he started to yell about why the hell did I feel the need to wake him up so early on a Saturday morning. I have learned over the years to ignore his choice in words, his attitude and his volume. I said your mother just called and we have to get to the hospital. One thing about Will is that he loves his mom and he sure nuff loves his brother. He jumped up right away and asked me what was wrong. I delivered the bad news. Will just sat stunned for a few minutes. How can this be? Abraham is only 34 years old and he has so much more living to do. I actually saw panic in my husband's eyes, and I knew then that he had the capacity to feel for someone other than himself. Hope arose. I always assumed that he loved his mother and brother, but this just confirmed it for me. My mind kept skipping to Sugar and how she was holding up. We had such hope for these two men. Lord, how can this be? Faith is the substance of things hoped for and evidence of things not seen. I caught myself. What is wrong with you? You are acting like Abraham is already in the casket and buried underground. You are a Christian and it ain't over until God says it is over. Where is your faith? I had to be strong and still believe that God would work this out in our favor.

Will and I quickly showered and changed our clothes. I woke up Faith and got her showered and dressed. Made some breakfast for her and then I heard the doorbell. I opened the door to let Darlene in and she quickly left with Faith. I looked for Will and I found him sitting on the bed staring into space. I called out his name and he was suddenly startled out of whatever world he was visiting. He got up, grabbed his keys and said let's go. I asked him if he wanted me to drive but he declined and said he was alright. Let me tell you, from the moment we entered the car until we landed at the hospital, I was praying up a storm. I thought the man was trying to do us in with his erratic driving. With his state of mind, as he drove, I knew better than to say a word. I just prayed.

We entered the hospital room to find Hannah and Sugar at Abraham's bedside. Abraham was hooked up to so many tubes that I lost count. He was fast asleep but every few minutes he would toss and turn and moan. Will and I exchanged hugs with his mom and sister-in-law. I asked Sugar if she had notified the church and asked them to intervene and offer up prayer on Abraham's behalf. She told me that she had spoken to the Pastor's wife, First Lady Naomi, and informed her about what was happening. First Lady said that she would inform the Pastor and that they would be praying for us. I was expecting Will to say something negative, but he never said a word nor did he make one of his famous facial impressions when the name of God is mentioned. He appeared to still be in shock.

He asked Sugar what happened. Sugar said that she had been asking Abraham to get a physical for so long that she grew weary in asking. She said that she had resigned herself to accept whatever hand she was dealt. She said that she saw that he was losing weight and not eating much. Sometimes he would be hunched over in pain, but the pain would pass, and he would go back to his original self. She said yesterday he was in so much pain that he was unable to go to work or make it out of bed. He was sweating and saying things that were clearly unintelligible. Against Abraham's wishes, Sugar said she called an ambulance. When they got to the hospital, they ran all kinds of tests and delivered the bad news a few hours ago. Sugar started to cry while saying that she refuses to become a widow by burying her husband. He was just too young. God, do you hear me, he is just too young.

CHAPTER- 3

Will and I didn't leave the hospital until 8 pm that night. We made a stop to pick up Faith and then we went home. Everyone was so exhausted. In spite of my weariness, I had to get my clothes ready for church in the morning. Just the thought of going to church was already lifting my spirits. You see, the only rock I know is Jesus and I needed His strength so much right now. I couldn't wait to enter the sanctuary with my fellow sisters and brothers and praise God despite whatever we were all going through.

One thing about God is that he does not discriminate in that everybody gets their own dose of problems. Part of life is how we deal with those problems. I choose to pray and lay my burdens down at God's feet. It is so good to know that I have a God who works tirelessly on my behalf. When I gather with the Saints or the Aint's as my husband would say, it is a re-affirmation of my faith. God not only comes through for me but for everyone else praising Him. He has the power to be everything to everyone everywhere all at the same time. My God is simply amazing. I didn't mean to go into this diatribe, but seriously, don't you ever look up at the sky and see the wonders of his power and marvel. I know I do. I guess he gives us all free will to decide how we want to live this life—with or without Him. It is so sad that people wait until calamity strikes to start searching for God. Better late than never I suppose.

I turn my attention to Will who is just sitting quietly in the darkened corner of the living room. I take Faith and get her ready for bed. She drifts off to sleep and I re-enter the outer room. I ask Will if he wanted something to eat and he told me no. Now that was a first. My husband is a notorious eater, one to eat you out of house and home. I knew that this situation was overwhelming him. I said Will, everything is going to be alright. Abraham is going to be ok. He said you sound so sure. I said that many prayers had been offered up for Abraham and I just cannot believe that those prayers will go unanswered and that premature death would be the final result.

He sat and listened. He then said that he was beginning to feel as if he is being punished for the way he has treated me during our marriage. How he made the connection between Abraham's illness and the state of our marriage is incredulous. The thought never even crossed my mind but if this is how I get some decent conversation, I'll take it. Will started to whisper that he always told Abraham that he would look out for him and now he felt so helpless and hopeless. I told him that we are all hopeless without God and that it is our faith in Him that truly gives us hope. I asked him to go to church with me in the morning. He refused but I could see that he paused and had actually considered it. Hope arose again. I told Will that God's arms are always open whenever he is ready. He thanked me for the invitation, and he said good night and proceeded to go to bed. I sat for a few minutes by myself just thanking God for this glimmer of hope. I cannot recall the last conversation I had with my husband where he ever contemplated for a second going to the house of God. Whoa. This is big God, this is really big.

CHAPTER- 4

At about 8 am, my eyes open up to the sound of running water. Will was already dressed and heading out the door to the hospital. He and Faith had eaten breakfast and he gave me a kiss on my cheek as he exited the house. Despite the present situation with Abraham, I felt an inner peace. He just had to be ok.

Faith and I got ready and left for church. When I entered the church, Living Christ International Church, I was filled with such an inner peace. I am not sure why I felt like I had been away for ages. The musicians were setting up the instruments, the saints were gathering in the sanctuary, some were kneeling and praying at the altar, some were sitting in Sunday school class, and the children were either engaged in spirited conversation or playing with one other. There was such joy and peace in the air.

Pastor Joshua took the altar and started to pray. This was code word for time to get ready for service. The praise and worship leaders then took the altar and the Choir took their positions. Songs of Praise started to permeate the atmosphere and I felt like I was in Heaven. No worries, no pain, no stress, all was well with me and with my soul. O how I love being in the presence of God with the rest of the saints, there is absolutely nothing like it. In his presence is where I give praise and worship and I receive blessings from on high in return. Some would say that it is an even exchange, but I beg to differ. My praise and worship pales in comparison to God's daily blessings. After all, who can beat God in giving, nobody I say, nobody at all.

Suddenly, my momma Esther popped into my mind. How happy she would be to see me serving the Lord. My momma always loved God and often spoke about his grace, his mercy and his goodness. As a young adolescent, I never wanted to hear anything about God. Growing up, my mother didn't go to church every Sunday, and in fact, we rarely ever went to church. But on Sunday's, only gospel music was played in our house and you would often find her reading her Bible and meditating on the Word when she wasn't drinking that is. You see, in my early years, my mother was two things, a great mom and also an alcoholic. I never blamed her because it must have been very difficult raising 4 children on your own with no one to help you carry that load.

You would hit the bottle too. She was the greatest mother in the world until she started drinking. Oh my God, talk about embarrassing. She would slur her words, stumble over herself, stagger all over the place and just be a plain embarrassment to her youngest daughter- yeah me. I remember how she loved Tab soda or so I thought. I would always be sent to the store to purchase the soda. She later admitted to me that she was putting liquor in the Tab soda. I had no idea.

At times when she would be sober, she would drag my brothers and I to the community tent revival church services. Whenever she got into this mode, it was so awful for us or so I thought. We had to go, no ifs, and ands about it. We were going. I remember rolling my eyes, sucking my teeth every time we were forced to attend those church services. I was certainly no believer in this God that they were speaking about and in fact I think that I just tuned out when I got there because to me, it was just a bunch of old people coming together. I was something else. Mom would just ignore us and continue to have a good time praising the Lord. If only Momma could see me now, she would have such a hearty laugh at my expense. She always knew the day would come when I would have to call on this same God. I never thought that day would ever come. But here we are. I can't get enough of this wonderful God. Wow. To think that I was so disrespectful and hateful towards God in my teenage years and he loved me despite my rudeness and in spite of myself. All I can say is Wow and thank you Lord.

Later on in life, my mother got it together and accepted the Lord Jesus Christ as her personal Savior. She stopped drinking and was baptized and went on to serve God with every fiber of her body. Unfortunately, the alcohol had already done its damage to her body and she suffered with diabetes and high blood pressure for the rest of her life. Although, she had to undergo dialysis on a weekly basis, nevertheless, she always said that God was good. She never missed an opportunity to tell people about God and his saving power. She ministered to people wherever she went. I used to hear her praying for the world, and I would marvel at her compassion. In those days, I had to get up enough stamina to pray for myself, the world and their problems were just too much for me to consider. But not my mama, she wanted the world to know that God was the answer.

I came back to my senses and reality and the choir and congregation was singing " O what peace we often forfeit, o what needless pain we bear, all because we do not carry everything to God in prayer." What an appropriate hymn for these circumstances. No matter what the problem or situation, we just need to take it to God in prayer and leave it there.

Lord, I have prayed for Abraham and I have prayed for Will and I leave these burdens with you. I refuse to carry these burdens back out with me, yep, I absolutely refuse. I am leaving them right here in this church with you Father God. Unlike me, you will know exactly what to do with them.

CHAPTER- 5

Faith and I came home to a darkened house. I was sure that Will would have reached out to me by now, but I have not heard anything. His cellphone is off. I hate when he does that. I am tired of telling him that I need to be able to reach him in cases of emergency. Who in the world needs to remind their husband of keeping his phone on? ME.

I walk in, put down my bag and fix something quick for us to eat. I hear Faith loudly playing in her bedroom. I sit down and all of a sudden, I feel so overwhelmed with sadness. I feel so alone. How can this be? I felt such peace while I was in the house of God and I now sit here with depression on the left and sadness on my right. I have to remind myself that all will turn out well. It is okay to feel despondent at times but not to dwell there. I remind myself that there is nothing too hard for God and He specializes in difficult situations. How can I minister healing to others when I too need healing?

Karma Will Clap Back

I immediately snap out of my downtrodden state and say to myself, O no Devil—the joy of the Lord is my strength, He will come through for me, He will never leave me nor forsake me and victory is already mine. Sometimes you have to encourage yourself, sometimes you have to speak to that mountain and force it to move. Mountain of doubt be moved in the name of Jesus, everything is going to be alright. At those moments where you are fighting for your Holy Spirit to rise, the Lord will always give you a song. The song He gave me was the hymnal "Victory is Mine" and I start to sing and hum, Victory is mine, victory is mine, victory today is mine, I told Satan, get thee behind, victory today is mine. When I woke this morning, I didn't have no doubt, I knew the Lord would bring me out, got down on my knees, said Lord help me please and then I got the victory. Wow, nothing like a good dose of an old-time song to get that Holy Ghost fire burning.

What was wrong with me? Can't beat myself up too much for being human. It is easy to become dismayed when looking at this situation with a natural eye, but I have learned that just because you don't see anything manifesting in the present does not mean that God is not working behind the scenes in the supernatural.

We walk by faith and not by sight. We believe in what we don't see, the supernatural, and we believe in that still small voice that we hear. I tell people that getting saved is as easy as just confessing with your mouth that Jesus is Lord and believing in your heart that God raised him from the dead. You can get saved right now just by confessing and believing that God raised Jesus from the dead. Getting saved is easy but the hard part comes in when you are trying to live this Christian life. It is as if the Devil says Oh yeah, you think I am just going to let you go so easily. No way, you will continue to serve me. So, there goes the war for your soul and the battle for your mind. I don't know about you, but Jesus has already won this battle. Keep on wasting your time Devil, I KNOW in whom I believe.

As I was having this conversation with the Devil, the door opened up and Will walked in and asked me who was I talking to on the telephone. I said I wasn't talking to anyone and he said that's strange since I clearly heard you talking to someone. I smirked, yeah that Devil. He said what? I said nothing Will, how is Abraham? He said he is still the same and pretty sedated. It is so hard to see my brother in that condition. People always feel as if they will live forever and that tomorrow is promised to them. How your life can change in a matter of seconds. I let him go on about how he and Abraham were supposed to conquer the world, and how they were going to chill out in their later years with their children and grandchildren swarming all around them. He talked about Momma Hannah and the grief and fear he sees when he looks into her face. How does one survive the loss of a child? I intervened to say Will, Abraham is not dead, and he will do whatever he has to do in order to survive.

Even if Abraham were to be taken away from all of us, I am not too worried about Momma Hannah since she is a prayer warrior and full of faith. She will be able to survive. I am not saying this will be easy for her but her trust in God will bring her through. Though I walk through the valley of shadow of death, I will fear no evil, for thou art with me, thy rod and staff they comfort me. Momma Hannah's God will continue to comfort her as she walks through this valley of shadow of death. What can I say, our faith in God allows us to find hope in what others would characterize as hopeless situations. Hopeless indeed.

CHAPTER- 6

Abraham slipped into a coma today. Sugar and Hannah were at his bedside praying when his body started convulsing and shaking. The nurses and doctors ran into the room and asked the family to leave the room. In a few minutes, they came out to tell the family that he had slipped into a comatose state. How can this be? Lord, are you hearing us? The many prayers we have offered up for Will and Abraham could fill up one third of heaven. Sugar just called to tell us the news. I asked her how Momma Hannah was holding up and she told me that she was holding on to God's unchanging hands. O Father God, where are we going with all of this?

I found Will in the bedroom with his hands under his chin and in a depressed state. He started to ask me about our God and where He was. He wanted to know what was the point of praying to a God that did not answer. I started to get hot and angry because don't nobody talk about my God and still live. Lucky for Will, my cooler self prevailed, and I said calmly that God does not operate on our time, but His timing is perfect. Will laughed and said, perfect for who, it ain't perfect for me. Boy, you are trying my last nerve.

I told him that God uses situations to teach us lessons and to bring about His purpose. Told Will that sometimes God use situations to bring us closer to Him. He muttered, the only way I will get close to Him is if he brings my brother out of this thing. Told him that he needs to love God for who He is and not what He can do for him. Will just shook his head and got up and went into Faith's room.

I sat there looking at his empty seat. God, please answer us. This is not supposed to end this way. Sugar, Abraham, Will and I were supposed to be chilling in our old days, watching the grandchildren run around while we laid back and relaxed on one of our porches. Premature death was not in the cards or so I thought. Girl, why are you thinking this way? Hey, what is your problem? It ain't over until God says it is over. Relax, take a chill pill. God is in control of this thing.

CHAPTER- 7

I woke up to the ringing phone. Of course, Will was fighting another battle with his nostrils and lungs and they were clearly winning. It was Sugar on the phone. She told me that Abraham woke up and he was going into surgery today. By the time we dropped Faith to school and got to the hospital, Abraham was already in the operating room. Will was in no rush to get to the hospital. He wanted to wait until the surgery was over before heading to the hospital. He believed that the anxiety at the hospital would kill him. My husband can be such a wimp at times. I finally convinced him to go to the hospital after a few hundred tries.

Upon arriving to the hospital, Momma Hannah, Sugar and I formed a circle and started to pray and call on our healer and deliverer. I was surprised when Will joined the circle by taking my hand as we all cried out to God. It didn't seem like it was too long before the doctors walked in to say that the surgery went well.

They believed that they were able to get all of the cancer out and that Abraham would have to undergo chemotherapy. We all exhaled and thanked the doctors. They said that it would be quite some time before Abraham would be able to return to the room. They suggested that we go and get some lunch and return in a few hours.

We formed another prayer circle and gave God thanks for answering our prayers. Momma Hannah and Sugar decided to stay in the room and wait for Abraham and Will and I decided to go and get something to eat. I told you that the man loves to eat.

Anyway, we went to a restaurant across the street from the hospital. When we sat down to dine, Will took my hand and told me that he loved me. Oh my God, I have not heard those words in ages. I started to tear up. God, what are you up to here? He apologized for how disrespectful he has been towards me and our marriage. He asked me, why do you stay with me? I told him because I believe in the vows that I took, and I believe in the God that I serve. God hates divorce and I know that He will turn my situation around. Without faith, it is impossible to please God, and my aim is to please Him. Will didn't say another word and I didn't either. I wanted to savor every second of the meal that God was serving. My husband joined a prayer circle and my husband told me that he loved me all in the same day. Go ahead God, do your thing.

When we returned to the hospital, and entered into the room, Abraham was sitting up, smiling and talking with Momma Hannah and Sugar. He was in some pain but still able to communicate. Will was so happy to see Abraham and Abraham was happy as well. Despite the pain, those two talked and laughed as if the rest of us were invisible. They had a bond for sure.

Momma Hannah said that the two siblings were always close like this even when growing up. She cannot remember a time that those two ever had an argument except for the time that they had a spat over Lady Cee. Could you imagine somebody naming their child Lady Cee? Well, she sure was something.

After school, she would give one of them her books and bags to carry. She would tell one to pick her up at one time and another one to pick her up at another time. Momma said that she would hear them arguing about who Lady Cee liked more and which one was taking her where on which particular day. One day Momma said she was in the kitchen when she overheard Will tell Abraham that this has got to stop. Supposed one of them ended up marrying her, there would be ill feelings and resentment towards the other one for life. Will said that they should both reconcile to leave Lady Cee alone for the sake of the brotherhood.

Abraham agreed and they both decided at that moment that they would never allow anyone or anything to come between them ever again. And to the best of her knowledge, they kept their promise to each other. No wonder Will feels powerless and helpless, sickness has come between him and his brother and there is nothing he can do about it this time. Except maybe appeal to the only person who might be able to help his brother—yes, Father God.

At some point they remembered that we were also in the room and they began to involve us in the conversation. Sugar seemed a bit weary today, so I took her downstairs to the hospital cafeteria for a cup of hot coffee. She thanked me for recognizing that she needed a few minutes away from the group. We had barely sat down for a minute before she started to express her fears. I listened and gave encouraging words, but I knew that I was failing miserably at comforting her.

I did the next best thing and I joined my hands with Sugar, and I began to pray to our Father in Heaven. For those who say that they don't know how to pray, prayer is just a conversation with God. He hears our prayers even if we don't speak it openly. I started the prayer by saying, Father, nobody knows how we really ought to pray, but it is your Holy Spirit that gives us the words to speak to you. I pray for Sugar and Abraham right now in the name of Jesus. Deliver them out of this trouble Lord and please make a way of escape for them. Let this situation not destroy but only strengthen them in the name of Jesus. We pray for Abraham's complete healing. We trust and believe that you have already sealed it in the name of Jesus. When we opened our eyes, Sugar had tears streaming down her face, but she said that she felt such an inner peace. Prayer will do it to you every time and every time prayer will do it.

We walked back into the hospital room and both men were munching on some of Momma Hannah's fine cooking. Although he seemed to still be in some pain, nothing was stopping Abraham from eating some of that food. They were both licking their fingers as if the food was going to disappear into thin air before they got every drop. Oh my, what a sight to behold. Momma Hannah interrupted all of the smacking lips to ask Sugar and I whether we wanted something to eat. I was amazed that Will was still hungry since we had just finished eating over at the restaurant across the street. I declined the food, but Sugar was famished. She indulged in the mean greens, potato salad and smoked turkey wings. Nothing like soul food to bring people together in the midst of a storm. If only we could stay in this moment of calm, but of course, the forces of reality would hear none of it. Reality struck back violently and regained its rightful position in our world. Here we go again.

Will's phone begins to ring, and he looked at the number and quickly put the phone on vibrate. If I tell you that his phone vibrated non-stop for ten minutes, trust me when I tell you that his phone vibrated for ten straight minutes. Momma Hannah shook her head and started to hum one of her hymns. How quickly the tide can change? It was obvious that it was one of his admirers wanting some attention from the man they hadn't heard from in a few days. Will looked embarrassed. That was surprising. Abraham closed his eyes as if he were suddenly the sleepiest man on Earth. What did I do or what did I want to do? I might as well tell you. I envisioned myself grabbing that cellphone out of his pocket and stomping on it, smashing it and throwing it against the wall. But I restrained myself, closed my eyes and asked God to help me to wait on Him and to fix this marriage before I ended up in the slammer or in the electric chair.

CHAPTER- 8

Even with the drama, Will and I left the hospital in a relatively good mood. I refuse to let anyone take away my peace or my joy. I can't account for how others want to live their life, but I want my life to be pleasing to God. On our way home, Will opened up by telling me that he planned to do better and that he wanted our marriage to work. He even said that he wanted to go to church with me on Sunday. I could not believe what I was hearing. Sometimes when God answers your prayers, it is indeed unbelievable. Sometimes it is instantaneous. What was unfolding before my eyes was truly incredible. We pulled up to our house and I was floating on high with excitement until I saw her.

In front of our home was an outraged, tall, slender, stunningly beautiful black woman. Will begged me to please stay in the car. I stayed partly because I was in shock and the other part of me wasn't sure what I would do if I exited the car. I had to think about my daughter Faith. How dare this woman come to my house? She knows where I live?

I must warn you that I have an altar ego by the name of Queen Jackie. She is in my head and there is nothing I can do about her. Believe me, I have tried. As I was saying, she knows where I live? Annoying voice in my head said, obviously girl, she is on your front lawn. Oh no, we really have a big problem now. I ain't nobody's punk. I feel the spirit of the Lord leaving me and that old person trying to rise up. Will is having a huge argument with this woman and she is not trying to hear whatever he is saying. How long does he want me to wait here? I have waited long enough. It is time to get out.

I exit the car and approach the lady arguing with my husband. I said may I help you and Will said I thought I told you to wait in the car. I told him that I had waited in the car long enough. I repeated my question to our guest, and she turned to me and said no, you cannot, with attitude. I told her that since I cannot help her then she really must leave my house. She said I came to speak with this gentleman. I said seems more like an argument than a conversation. I then asked her for her name. She said "Sweet Caroline" is my name. Oh boy, here we go. I am not going to jail. I picked up my phone and dialed 9-1-1. When they answered, she got the gist and walked off but not before pointing to my husband and letting him know that they had some unfinished business. Lord, really? You gave me such great hope today and now this? I hear the spirit of God saying weeping may endure for a night, but joy comes in the morning. Well Spirit of God, you are surely telling the truth, for I am going inside my house to weep this night away.

CHAPTER- 9

I am sitting in the bathroom in complete shock. How could he do this to me? How could he let one of his admirers know where we lived? I feel so stupid and ashamed at the same time. How could I expect God to fix this unfixable situation called my marriage? I feel as if I am the stupidest person on the Earth right now. How much more disrespect can I tolerate from this man? The audacity of this woman to show up at my home. Lord, help me to make it through the night. I am so upset. All of a sudden, I hear a knocking on the door. Before I could answer, Will entered the bathroom. He said that he was sorry for what I had witnessed and that he had made some poor choices in the past that he was trying to correct. He told me that the woman's name was Caroline and that he had been seeing her off and on for a year. He said that he broke it off with her recently and she is not happy as I clearly witnessed. He asked for my forgiveness and asked me to please give him another chance to make this marriage work. I literally couldn't believe my ears, but I certainly believed my eyes. Caroline's face kept appearing before me and I couldn't get her out of my head. Tell me about it said Queen.

I asked Will about the sudden change and why should I take him seriously. He said that Abraham's sickness gave him a jolt and made him realize that life is too short, and he has to take accountability for his actions. He continued by saying that he would not want anyone to mistreat his daughter and karma has a way of visiting its evil upon your children. He said that he loved me, and he wanted our marriage to work. He promised to be a better husband to me and less selfish.

This man looks like my husband and talks like my husband, but is it my husband? I looked at Will and I really felt as if he was being sincere. Some people might say that I was crazy for believing him after what transpired but God takes the foolish things of this world to confuse those who think that they are so wise. To be completely honest, I am not overly concerned about what people think or else I would have divorced Will a long time ago. What is God up to? This day has been oh so draining for me, filled with ups and downs.

I thanked Will for expressing his thoughts and I told him that I would come to bed shortly, but I needed a few minutes of alone time. When Will left, I started to praise God in song, and I started to utter words of thanksgiving. With God, things can happen in the twinkling of an eye. How fast things can turn around? Not calling 11 years fast Lord, but your timing is perfect. I sat in the bathroom in disbelief. Could he be toying with me? Sure, but what would be the point? I believe him and given the reaction of Sweet Caroline, she believes him too. Bye sweet Caroline, it's over hun.

CHAPTER- 10

Did I say over? Well, maybe over for Will but Caroline obviously had other ideas. I woke up to a ringing phone. Something told me that it was not good news. I picked up the phone to hear a woman on the phone asking to speak with Will. I immediately recognized the voice. Caroline, what can I do for you? I would like to speak to Will. I am sorry but Will is sleeping. She had the nerve to ask me to wake him. I told her that I was not planning to do so. She started cursing and ranting about how I did not want to mess with her. I told Caroline that she needed to find God and to leave my husband alone. That is not going to happen, we are tied to each other for a very long time. He should have thought about doing the right thing before he planted his seed in my stomach. You see Karma, our son is a year old. I will not allow that man to throw me to the side as if I am some sort of insignificant garbage. Not going to happen, so you tell your husband that he had better make this right.

I held the phone in my hand as she was talking but I had travelled back in my mind to our wedding day. We were going to take the world by storm. We had enough love for the whole world. As I stood there, I came back from reminiscing and realized that I had tears streaming down my face. Will walked into the room and took the phone out of my hands. He must have heard her voice and he hung up the phone.

I turned to my husband, the one I had given my heart to and the one that I had pledged to love forever, and I had no more words left. Will asked me what Caroline said to me and I just couldn't speak. I just slumped down to the floor and rocked myself like you would a baby. I can't tell you how long I was in that position. I heard Will speaking and I felt him shaking me, but I had disappeared so deep inside myself that I am not sure that I could have found my old self if I had tried.

I can't describe the feeling of betrayal by the one who is supposed to love and protect you. I can't describe the hurt, the pain, the anger, the resentment, and the fury. I can't describe what it feels like to have your heart broken in two and then shattered into pieces. In my pain, I heard my daughter Faith's voice and I felt her touch. She said Mama, are you okay? Mama, you are scaring me. Something inside of me awakened and I turned to look at my beautiful angel, I had to fight for her. I had to keep it together for her sake and for mine. I began to pray and to ask God to please help me. I couldn't find the words, but in my moaning and groaning, I know that God understood.

A child. Will has a child and it is not my child. Rumors have now been confirmed. Faith said Mama, I am hungry. I came to once again and immediately went into mommy mode and found the strength to make her something to eat. She then went into her room to play and I went back to the problem at hand. Will has a child and it is not my child. God, you have now given me the opportunity to walk out of this joke of a marriage. The sound of freedom is so appealing at this moment. I can't think of being tied down to a man that I don't know anymore. Who is this person?

Will walked into the room and asked me if I were okay. I asked, what do you think?. He then asked me what was wrong and what did Caroline say to me. I turned to my husband and asked him if he had something to tell me. He looked at me for about 10 seconds and I could see tears in his eyes. He said Yes, Karma. I wish I could change my mistakes, but I can't. Karma, at some point, I lost my way. The grass looked greener on the other side and I dipped into waters that I should have avoided. Yes, I should have told you a year ago, but I just couldn't find the words.

Karma, I have a one- year old son by Caroline and his name is Imani. I stayed out of the house so much because I couldn't deal with the guilt every time I looked at you or looked at Faith. I know that I don't even deserve your forgiveness, but I am hoping that you will show me mercy and forgive me.

I don't know why it has taken my brother's illness to open my eyes to the things that are important in life. Do you love her? No. I am not in love with Caroline. Will, how can we move on from here? Please tell me. I am so lost right now. Just looking at you is so hard for me right now. I feel like throwing things, I feel like screaming, I feel like just giving up on life. Betrayal by someone you trusted can be a life ending exercise. You just don't feel like going on anymore. You go through so many emotions and you are just ready to throw in the towel and give up on life. But God. Even in low moments like these, I have to reach deep inside of me and trust God since he has never failed me yet. This situation is not any different. I know that I can, and I will triumph over the enemy. I know that I can face any challenge that comes my way and emerge with the victory. God says yes, I can, and I believe Him.

Back to Will. He said I don't expect you to stay with me after all of this. I have messed up so badly that I don't know how I will ever be able to move forward. I just don't know what more to say Karma, but I am so sorry for hurting you and destroying our family. I hope that you can find it in your heart to forgive me and at least be my friend. I really need a friend at this time. Queen Jackie said friend, did your husband say that he hopes that you two can remain friends. Is he serious? With friends like him, why would you need enemies? I can't stand these trifling men. I shrugged off Queen Jackie's comments and looked at Will's face.

Can you imagine, I am supposed to be the mad one and I am feeling sorry for this man. I think about God's grace and how often we all mess up and God still forgives us. I hear the words of the Lord's prayer, forgive those who trespassed against you so that your Heavenly Father can forgive you your trespasses. If you can't forgive, why would Father God forgive you when you trespass against Him. We are all imperfect beings and so it is a sure thing that you will trespass against Father God. Queen retorted, Oh Karma, are you for real? This man has done you dirty, how in the world can you forgive him? I hear the argument going on in my head. How? I don't know how but I know that I must do so. I intend to make it into Heaven, and nothing is going to stop me from getting there, including you Queen. It may take a while for me to completely heal, but God will help me through this storm.

I look at Will and tell him I am not sure what I am going to do but I am sure in time that he will have my forgiveness. He seemed relieved and thanked me for even thinking about forgiving him. I told him forgiveness did not mean that we would remain married but at least my heart would be clean where he was concerned. I actually heard him say that he had been praying to God and asking for forgiveness. I asked for some alone time and he quietly left the room. Karma girl, what is your next step? Self, I wish I knew the answer to that question.

CHAPTER- 11

I woke up the next day just wanting to praise God. I thanked him for keeping my mind and for giving me the strength to move forward. I thanked God for showing me that it was possible to extend love even at a time when I was experiencing such brokenness. Father God, I love you and I want to know that I am doing your will. What is your will when it comes to my marriage? Should I stay or leave? I have been hurting for so long that I just want this pain to end. I hear the Lord saying that there is more that He requires of me and that it is never His will for any to divorce. He said I gave the bill of divorcement because of the hardness of men's hearts especially in the area of infidelity. I hear the Lord saying, you can leave the marriage Karma and it is entirely permissible but think about what happens if you stay and you persevere and stand on my Word and trust me to make this situation right again. Do you see how your husband is turning to me in the midst of this storm? Don't question my methods, just trust me to work it out for you. God, I will trust you. After all, you thought I was worth saving and you sacrificed your life to save me. The least I can do is to trust you. You thought I was worth dying for, you cleaned me up and now I am free. I want everyone to know this freedom even in the midst of their storm. I want others to feel this assurance that I have. I want everybody to know that God is always with them and He will work out every adverse circumstance in your life. Glory. I have to praise and worship this God. I was dancing around my room, praising and singing melodies to God. Hallelujah to the God who changed my life. Anybody who saw me would have thought that I was crazy. Yes, crazy for Jesus. Every praise belongs to God and I am giving Him his glory. What a privilege and honor to praise and worship this God even in the midst of the valley. Praise him until you reach your mountaintop.

The more I praised, the better I felt. I wish those naysayers would just try it. Don't knock it until you try it. God is real. Through the praises, I was able to see clearly the positive changes my husband had been making in the last couple of weeks. I was able to lift up my hands and give God all the glory for the things He was doing. Either I am going to trust you God, or I might as well walk away from this whole Christian walk and I am not going to do that for no-one. No more tears, I cried my last tear yesterday. I trust you

God. Now tell me, what is our next step. Just follow me daughter, I will show you.

CHAPTER- 12

I felt the urgent need to call Momma Hannah. It felt so good to hear a familiar voice other than that of Caroline playing and echoing in my head. I explained to Momma Hannah why I have been absent from the hospital for the last few days and exactly what had transpired since I last saw her. She sat silently as I unfolded the dirty linen of my marriage and spilled all of the business. Momma Hannah said that she knew that something was wrong, and she knew that we were struggling, but she prayed and placed it in God's hands. After all, there is no perfect marriage and if someone says their marriage is perfect, you can tell them that I said that they are a big fat liar and in denial.

Momma Hannah asked me whether I had made any decisions concerning the marriage. I told her I had not, but I was putting my trust in the Almighty. It suddenly hit me that I had not even asked about Abraham and his condition. Momma said that he was recovering and getting stronger every day. I was so engrossed in my own problems that I did not even remember about Abraham and Sugar. Their problem was one of life and death; this problem hurts but it won't kill me. Momma Hannah said that she had a story to tell me. She told me that she had never uttered a word of this to anyone and she hoped that I would keep her confidence.

She started to talk about Will and Abraham's father, John. They rarely spoke about him. He died when the boys were very young. Momma said that they used to call him Papa John, but the man was surely a rolling stone. He had so many women that it shamed her now to think that she ever laid down with that man. Momma Hannah said that she loved the ground that the man walked on and she would have done anything to keep him all to herself.

Unfortunately, he would and could not be contained. The man just loved women, ugly, pretty, light, dark, fat, skinny, breathing, not breathing. She said that she was so distraught when he left her that she wanted to take her own life. But she thought about her two small kids and didn't know what would happen to them if she gave in to her depressed state of mind. Momma Hannah said that she remembered the exact day that she contemplated suicide as if it were yesterday. She said that she was home in her kitchen when he walked into the house. He went into the room and packed his bags hurriedly. He quickly came out of the room and looked at me and said that he was moving to Atlanta, Georgia. I thought he was joking but the bags in his hand told me that this was no joke. I said how, why, what about the children? He said they would be fine. Hannah, don't you see that all of the children around here don't have fathers around, stop making a big deal out of this. Look, I didn't have my father around and I turned out alright. I wanted to laugh and scream at the same time. You turned out alright, I asked.? He continued by saying Hannah, you knew the type of man that I was from the beginning. I need to breathe, and I feel like I am being stifled. I was amazed that the father of my children could be so cold-hearted and callous.

I don't know what made me look out of the window at that exact moment but sure enough there she was. Nice, beautiful, curvaceous and naive. Lord, I recognized myself immediately in her. I wanted to tell her to run for her life and don't turn back but what's the use, she would never have listened. She was going along for the ride until the road said dead end. If I had only listened to my parents and my friends, life would have been so very different. He walked out the door and we didn't hear from him except for one solitary time when he tried to creep back in. His sister called me up a few years after that last encounter to tell me that he had died. I just felt sorry for him in that he was a lost soul.

After he left the apartment that day, I cried and cried and cried. My kids would come into the room and I would just lie there staring into space. I am not even sure how they survived those first few days after their father abandoned us. I was in my own world and I just wanted to die. I thought about taking some pills. Everybody was right about him and I felt so used and stupid. I just didn't want to face life anymore.

Momma Hannah continued, one morning, I heard a knock on my door, and I scrambled to go and get it. There was a lady at the door, and she identified herself as Sister Mary. She said that she had just moved into the neighborhood and she felt her spirit forcing her to come and knock on the door and tell whoever opened the door about the goodness of Jesus. I wanted to slam the door in her face. I only gathered the energy to make it to the door because I thought it could possibly be my man coming back to say that he had made a giant mistake and wanted to ask for my forgiveness.

Instead, at the door, I find a Bible thumping lady coming to interrupt my misery. She looked at me and said Chile, ain't no man worth all that. I said what are you talking about? She said I been around the block long enough to recognize man trouble and ain't no earthly man worth all of that. Pull yourself together for the sake of your children, I know he done left you with some. When will women recognize that God's way is the only way? God said to wait until you are married before you give away the goods and all you women just open up and spread your legs wide and let these men buy the goods without putting down a penny. I wanted to slap this woman, but she was making sense and funny too.

She said ma'am I don't know you from Adam, but I want to tell you that Jesus saves. God is real and so is His Word. All of that energy you spending on that trifling man should be the same energy you spend on your children and on learning about God. She said I was in the same boat many years ago and I thank God that through the pain I was able to rise up and get myself together for my children. Kids need both parents but if one parent decides that they are not going to be there, my God I hope the other will be there to pick up the pieces.

She asked me the last time that I had taken a bath and I couldn't tell her. She took my hand and prayed for me. She asked God to renew my strength and to save my soul. Half of what she was saying I didn't understand, I guess it was her prayer language. She then pushed her way into my apartment and ordered me to jump in the shower. She proceeded to tidy up the house and called the children out of the room and fixed them a proper meal.

Jacqueline Greene

When I came out of the shower, I felt like a weight had been lifted off of me. The world and my outlook on life looked much brighter. Who was this lady? Her name was Evangelist Mary Cooke. She turned out to be a spiritual mother to me until she went to be with the Lord a few years back.

One of the things that I learned from that sweet woman of God was to always place God first in my life. We should never worship men, yes, we should love our men and our husbands, but we must not worship them or allow them to mistreat us. Men must respect their wives. Momma Hannah said that she was so disappointed in Will's actions, but I must not wallow in defeat since I did nothing wrong. She said that she could not say what she would do in my situation but there is nothing too difficult for God. Momma told me to hold on to God's unchanging hands and to continue to pray for clarity and God will show me the way.

She said that about one year after John had abandoned her and the children, he showed up at her door with his bags. I guess the beautiful girl waiting on the corner had finally come to the end of her road with him. He begged Momma Hannah to allow him to stay and told her how he had mended his ways. Momma Hannah said she just looked at him pitifully and told him that he needed

Momma Hannah

to find the Lord. She told him to have a good night and she closed her door.

At that point in her life, she had found Jesus and she was not about to let him go for some rolling stone who didn't have a home. Momma Hannah said that she was so proud of herself when she shut that door on ole John. I say all this to say to you Karma that I cannot tell you what to do. Will is my son and you are my daughter and I don't want to sanction your pain, but I don't know what the future will hold. Only God does. So, in this regard, you really have to turn down your plate and seek the face of God. Some things will not change except for fasting and praying. I was able to let ole John go because God had already shown me what true love looked like and that sure as hell wasn't it. I love you Karma, but you will have to put on your big girl panties and make this difficult decision. Trust that God will answer your prayers in due time and your path will become patently clear. I thanked Momma Hannah for her guidance and direction, and I hung up the phone feeling somewhat let down. I always depended on Momma Hannah for direction but this time she could not direct me instead she sent me to the Director Himself. I got down on my knees and began to pray and talk to God.

Father God, I need you to hear me and to answer me. I don't know whether I am supposed to stay in this marriage or leave. I know that you can turn any situation around and I have been waiting patiently for this marriage to turn around, and just when I thought we were heading in a positive direction, all hell has broken loose. I heard this small voice saying, isn't that how it usually is? When you are about to get a major breakthrough, all the forces of hell will come together to stop your progress. I reasoned with God. Yes God, but I am only human, how much of this am I expected to endure? Daughter, when your victory is near or your prayer is about to be answered, the battle gets a bit intense, but my grace is sufficient. Lord, I just don't feel like I can take any more of the disrespect. Get out of your feelings Karma and grow up. It is time for you to digest the Word and really put it into action. Nobody said the road would be easy, but it will be worth it in the end. Are you so blinded by your feelings that you can't see the changes your husband has made within the twinkling of an eye? This Christian life is not about feelings. If it were about feelings, my beloved Son would have given up and gone back to Heaven instead of enduring the shame and pain for you Karma, for Will, for Faith, even for sweet Caroline as she likes to call herself. I came for souls and I use people like you Karma who believe and trust me to work difficult situations out.

I love it when my children boast about me and have faith in my power to set them free. You were doing so well Karma, what happened? My husband just admitted to me that he fathered another woman's child, that is what happened, but you already know. Yes Karma, I know but why has that changed your faith in me. I know that you can turn this around God, but the question is whether I want you to do it. Really Karma, after eleven years of hearing you pray, whine, beg, cry, throw tantrums, make lame jokes about my timing, now is when you want to abandon the ship? People really must think about what they want before they start praying and asking for things. My ways are not your ways Karma and the way I accomplish things is the way that I choose to do it. Are you now like your brother Job questioning how I do things? I am God, did you forget? No God, I did not forget. I guess it is kind of crazy when you put it that way. Yes, crazy indeed. Alright God, thank you for talking with today and for providing your infinite wisdom and guidance. Sure thing daughter, you know that I am always here for you. Yes Abba, I know.

CHAPTER- 13

I got up off of my knees to find Will standing in the doorway. He asked me who was I talking to. I wondered how much of my conversation did he hear. I said God. He said Oh. He asked me whether I was ready to talk to him. I said okay although I still couldn't bear to look at him. Help me God. I will, daughter. Karma, I am so sorry that I hurt you and I wish I could turn back the hands of time, but I can't. I messed up badly and I hope in time that you will be able to forgive me. Will, I am sure in time that I will be able to forgive you. I am just not sure when that will happen or how it will happen. Do you want me to move out? Will, I don't believe in running from problems but facing them head on. We have to work through this problem in hopes of repairing our marriage.

I couldn't believe what was coming out of my mouth. Am I really going to try to save this marriage? Girl, you stupid was the loud, obnoxious voice in my head belonging to the one and only

Queen. Will looked at me with tears in his eyes, you really think that we can work this out in spite of my infidelity. Yes Will, I think that we can. He motioned for a hug and I reluctantly gave him one. Girl, what is wrong with your dumb self. I can't believe I am stuck in a stupid body. Loud and obnoxious voice again in my head. Will and I hugged for what felt like an eternity, it reminded me of the old days. He asked me whether I wanted to discuss anything with him. I told him that we would have plenty of time to discuss all of this, but I just wanted to take my mind off of us and call Sugar and see how she was doing. My husband agreed and I dialed Sugar's number.

Sugar picked up immediately and I asked her how she was doing. She replied that she was ok, but I knew that she was still not ok. It must feel horrible to have your husband laid up in a hospital and you cannot do anything to assist or alleviate any of his pain. Sugar said that her husband was indeed doing better than expected and that he was going home soon. I thanked God for answered prayer and all of my problems paled in comparison to the life and death problem facing Sugar and her husband. I told her that we would be there tomorrow to see them, and we said our good-byes. I wonder if Sugar knew about Will's baby and chose not to get involved. Nope, my girl wouldn't withhold such important information from me. Or would she?

I turned to Will and I told him that in order for our relationship to heal and to move forward, we have to be completely honest with one another. He agreed and told me that he wanted to come clean about everything since he was hoping for a fresh start. I asked him about Caroline and their initial encounter. He told me that she was someone that he met at work. It started off with light flirting which turned hot and heavy really quickly. He said that he did not expect Caroline to go away quietly and that he might lose his job over all of this. She threatened to report him to his bosses and to tell everyone about their affair. He said that he has tried to reason with her for the sake of Imani, but she is not having it. Will said that she is refusing to let him see his child.

When he said those words, I felt like someone had kicked me in my stomach. He must have noticed the look and pain in my face because he immediately apologized for being so callous. I told him that I am a big girl and the child has nothing to do with the situation except that he is a byproduct of the relationship. I asked him whether he was thinking about going to court. He said only with my blessing. I told him that he has my blessing in that children need both parents in their lives.

I asked Will, why? He told me that, although no excuse will ever be good enough, he felt bored and trapped. He said that sex between us had become routine and robotic and he wanted more excitement. I asked him why did he not discuss his feelings with me? He didn't know how expressing those thoughts would have changed things for the better. He could see me blowing up and getting mad. How do you tell your wife, I am bored in this marriage? I asked him, what has changed? I am the same person. He said Karma, I know you are the same person, but I am not. I am the one who has changed. My family is more important than satisfying my lower half. I wish I had learned this lesson earlier, but I cannot go back, I can only go forward. I know that I will need help and I am willing to ask for it where necessary. I have even started praying and asking God to help me. I feel as if he hears me when I pray and that is very encouraging. I know that I am not alone. Just the fact that you are talking to me shows that the man upstairs is already answering my prayers. I am clearly not perfect Karma, but I am more than happy to change my ways.

Will, I can't sit here and tell you that I am not hurting. I am torn and bleeding profusely. I am not sure I know how to stop the pain or how to stop the bleeding, but I am trusting God. Nothing worth having ever comes easily and I believe that my marriage is worth fighting for. All I can say is that I am willing to try. I have waited so long to hear the words that you are speaking, and I just hope that it is not too late for us. I took vows to love you in sickness and in health and in good times and bad. We are facing bad times at the moment, but I keep telling myself that this too shall pass. Trouble don't last always. Or does it?

CHAPTER 14

The phone woke me up. It was about 5 am on a Saturday morning. I was not running to answer the phone given my last experience with Caroline. Whenever I answer these early morning calls, it is never good. Phone keeps ringing. Will is in his own world and nothing will disturb him until he is ready to come out.

I gather the courage to get up and answer the phone. Not to disappoint but there she was again. I said what can I do for you? She said you can't do anything for me, but Will can. I wanted to jump through the phone and take her out of her misery. Lord, help me with this lunatic. I asked again, why are you calling my house? She said you know why I am calling. I said I really don't know why you insist on dialing my number when Will has a cellphone, call him on it. She said I would, but he is not answering it. Maybe that should tell you something since it is 5 am in the morning and he is not answering because he is asleep.

Try him later and I hung up the phone. It felt so liberating to hang up on her. It might not have been the Christian thing to do but Lord, this lady is trying my last nerve.

Phone started ringing again. I wonder if I will have to file harassment charges on this heifer. I pick up the phone and she apologized for calling the house so early. I listened since she was finally acting like she bought some sense. She said that she was calling to tell Will that his son was involved in a little accident a few days ago. Oh boy, I can feel the baby mama drama starting. Why did you not call him on his phone? She said I have been calling him for days, but he won't answer the phone.

Caroline, I am sorry about your son, but do you realize that Will is a married man and he wants to stay married. He cannot stay married if he continues to have communication or relations with you. That is the reason why he is not answering his phone.

He said that he told you that it is over, but you are not quite understanding his language, so let me try to help you out. My marriage will survive this affair. This incident will not break our union. You really need to find somebody else to harass because it will not be me. I am not sure how this will play out since we have an innocent child in the midst, but I am confident that my husband will take care of his responsibilities and provide for his son.

I couldn't believe the words that were coming out of my mouth. Apparently, my alter ego, Queen Jackie couldn't either since all I could hear was stupid, stupid, stupid, all up in my head. I told my alter ego, you must really stop all of this negativity. She said you really must stop being naive and stupid. I think Queen Jackie, we will have to lay down some ground rules. You only speak when spoken to or speak when I ask for your opinion. Oh no Karma, that is not how this thing works. They call me Queen because I rule, and I don't take orders from anybody. Oh boy, another drama queen.

I stopped talking to the other me and returned back to my conversation with Caroline. She said I think it would help if he came to see his son. Caroline Will told me that you were refusing to let him see his son. She said I was, but I could tell that he misses his father. I wonder what kind of woman keeps her son away from their father willingly. She said she understands that Will has somehow found a new lease on life and wants to save his marriage. She asked me to please have him come to Columbia General to see his son. I told her that I would convey the message and she thanked me and hung up the phone.

I sat in the dark for quite some time, not sure how many hours went by. I was startled when Will came into the room and asked me if I were okay. I told him that I was still grappling with the fact that he has a child and it is not mine. I started to cry, and he came and hugged me and said he was so sorry for hurting me. I told him that I was really doing my best to move forward but every time I make two steps forward something pulls me back down into the pit.

I turned to him and said that Caroline called to tell him that his son was in the hospital and she thought it would be helpful if he came to see him. I could see the alarm in my husband's eyes, and it was like somebody kicked me in my stomach. I had to remember that we were talking about an innocent child here. Poor baby. I had to come to grips with the fact that my husband has a child that is not mine and he will be responsible for this child for many years to come. I have to choose which route I am going to take. Either I can choose to embrace the child , or I can choose to separate myself and Faith from this innocent child.

I hear Queen Jackie saying are you trying to qualify for sainthood? This is ridiculous. What woman does this? Why do you have to deal with his shame every day of your life? If you choose to stay, which is crazy, but if you choose to stay, why embrace the sin? I am not embracing the sin. I am choosing to forgive my husband and embrace his child.

Queen said you do realize that you are also embracing Caroline and her child, don't you? Of course, I am not stupid. Queen quipped, you could have fooled me. Lord, help me with this voice in my head. My alter ego said you can call me all the names you want to call me, but you are being foolish. I responded, okay, let me be foolish. She responded, and it wouldn't be so bad if I didn't also have to live through it. I said, you don't have to live through it, you can just go away. She responded, I am afraid that can't happen. I am inside of your head and did you forget that I am considered your sensible side. Don't know what you would do without me. Queen Jackie, you are so funny, but I would sure like to find out how life would be without you all up in my business.

Back to my conversation with Will. Husband, I can't fake the funk and act like this is not affecting me. It hurt like hell. Will said that he wants to build back my trust and he will have to tell me things that he knows might hurt me. I told him that I prefer him to be honest. He said that he is torn since he does not want to hurt me, but he cannot abandon his son. He said that he was contemplating taking Caroline to court for visitation rights but didn't know how to approach the subject with me.

I told him that maybe that will be unnecessary since she was clearly asking him to come and see the child. He asked me if I would go with him. I sat there pondering this in my head. One voice said no and the other said of course you should. I turned to him and said that I would try my best to get to the point one day where I can interact freely with his son, but I just can't do it right now. That voice in my head said finally she got some sense. He said that he understood, and he is hoping that I can get there one day. I told him that I was hoping to get there one day soon. He hugged me and kissed me before getting ready to go to the hospital. I wondered about whether I made the right decision. He was surely going to be alone with the mother of his child and Lord knows what will happen. I conjure up scenes and pictures in my head of them kissing and getting down and dirty. The inner voice said yep, sense has finally arrived. I tried to erase the images out of my head. I called on God to help me get through this moment. All of a sudden, I felt His inner peace overtake me. I felt calm and I knew that it was okay to take my time to get to the point where I could fully trust my husband.

I thought about how many times I have messed up in my life and God forgave me. I thought about the spotless Lamb who came to give His life for this sinful world and to save us all. Glory to the

Lamb that takes away the sin of the world. He is the King of Kings and Lord of Lords. We give glory to the Lamb of God for the great things He has done. Glory to the One who takes away the sins of this world. Father God, cleanse my heart from all unrighteousness and create in me a clean heart. Use this experience to teach others that you are alive and well and marriages can be saved when we forgive each other their trespasses as you continue to forgive us. If I can't weather this storm, then how can I witness to an unbeliever or believer who is suffering in their marriage? How can I tell them that God will make a way if I can't see through my pain and see the cross and know that deliverance is ahead. I choose to believe God and stand in the midst of my pain knowing that He has already made the way. Hallelujah!!

I felt His peace overtake me again. I quickly got up and went into my room to get ready. My husband looked up when I entered the room. I told him that I changed my mind and that I would accompany him to the hospital. He seemed relieved for some reason. Maybe he didn't want to face Caroline alone. Anyway, I hurriedly put on my clothes and makeup and we were out the door with Faith. I dropped her off at my girl Darlene's house and I told her that I would explain later. I felt armed and ready to take on the world with my husband at my side. Glory be to God! Hospital, here we come.

CHAPTER- 15

We got to Columbia General in no time. For once, my mind was not even focused on Will's driving, but I was thinking about what we were about to face. We entered the hospital and we were directed to Imani's room. When we entered the room, Caroline was sitting there holding her son's hands. She smiled when she saw Will, but the smile quickly disappeared when she realized that I was with him. She asked, what is she doing here? He said, she is my wife and I asked her to come. She said, "you weren't calling for your wife" when you were in between my parts. I want her to leave now. I said, "Caroline, I am not going anywhere, you asked me to give Will the message and I did, and he is here to look about the welfare of his son." All of a sudden, I heard a young voice crying dada, dada. The child was so cute, he looked exactly like a young version of my husband. I had so many emotions going through me at the same time; I felt pain, relief, compassion, empathy and yes, love. I was so torn and afflicted and I stood motionless as Will reached for his son's hands. Caroline just stared and rolled her eyes at me and Will ignored her and asked her what happened. She sucked her teeth and said that the child was playing on the bed and before she knew it, he had taken a serious tumble onto the floor. He asked her what the doctors said. Caroline said that they had taken X-rays and that she was waiting for the results. She said this was the first time that Imani seemed alert.

I even had compassion for Caroline, after all, it is definitely heart wrenching for a mother to have a bed ridden child in the hospital. What must she be going through? There goes that alter ego of mine. What is wrong with you? Lord, have mercy girl. The woman wants to take your man and you are here wondering about how she is feeling. She is feeling like she wants to kick your stupid behind. How about that? How much plainer must I make it, she wants to take your husband away from you. Wake up and smell the flowers that are lying in front of you. Lord, be like me, why don't you just tell her off. I shrug off the voice when I see the doctor walk into the room. The doctor said that the x-rays came back negative and Imani would be okay. He had a slight sprain on his left leg, but they would wrap it up and release him shortly. I could see that Will was slightly relieved that his son would be discharged. Caroline breathed a huge sigh of relief and started again with her antics regarding my presence at her son's hospital bed. She asked me, why in the world did I come? I told her because I wanted to support my husband. She said you must be one stupid heifer. I hear my alter ego saying, uhumm, I could see that insult coming. But you want to live in this dream world where everybody is so good. This woman is not your friend, nor does she want to have anything to do with you.

Will intervened and told Caroline that the only reason he is here is because I told him that I supported his coming to the hospital. He told her that he is sorry for hurting her and he has told her many times that he loves his wife and intends to save his marriage. Caroline just looked at him with tears in her eyes and she said, now is when you decide that you have a moral bone in your body? Now is when you decide that you love your wife? Now is when you decide that you want to save your marriage? What am I supposed to do with the child that you have left me with? He said Caroline, it is over, and I am very sorry but I cannot live a lie. I hope that God will forgive me my transgression as well as my wife. Imani is a beautiful child and you are blessed to have him. Caroline looked at Will and stated that it was never her desire to be a single mother. Will said Caroline, I am sorry. I don't know what else to say to you to make this right. Caroline looked at me and said that I really picked a winner of a husband and just know that he will never change. I refused to respond with bitterness, but I told her that I understood all that she was feeling. She just glared at me and said that I will never understand what she is feeling.

The doctor and nurse came back into the room, wrapped up Imani's legs and gave Caroline the discharge papers. Imani reached for Will and Will picked him up and gave him a big kiss on his forehead. The child was beaming as he looked into the eyes of his father. Again, I felt like someone had kicked me in the gut and head at the same time. Will looked over at me and asked me whether I was alright. I told him that I was, and he said okay, just checking.

Caroline walked out of the room and we followed her to her car. As Will was putting Imani in the car seat, the child began to cry for Will. I could see the pain in my husband's face as he told his son that he would come by to see him soon. Caroline yelled at the child to be quiet and she stormed away to open up her car door. Before she got into the car, Will asked her to give him a good time for him to visit with Imani? She said that he can come tomorrow, but don't dare bring me to her house. Will said that maybe they can meet at a mutual spot for him to visit with his son. Caroline opened her car door and said that it would be her house or no place at all. She then started her engine and off in the wind went Sweet Caroline. O Lord, what in the world are we in for? Why can't these disputes settle outside of court? Why do people always forget about the love or lust that they once shared and let bitterness rule their hearts when relationships turn sour? Unfortunately for us, Family Court, here we come.

CHAPTER- 16

So, we arrived at the lawyer's office the very next morning. The lawyer told Will that he would first seek a paternity test and then depending on the results, Will would have to start paying child support. Will said he already came to grips with the reality of his son and he was prepared to take full responsibility for his actions. The lawyer looked at me and asked me whether I was ready for the fight ahead. I told the attorney that I wished there was another solution, but the lady was incensed and would not budge from excluding me from the equation.

The lawyer, his name was Judah, said that he commended me for standing with my husband. I thanked him and told him that it was only by the grace of God that I was able to continue moving forward. Will looked at me and kissed my hand and whispered thank you. Judah said that he would file the papers tomorrow and he would get back to us with the court date and the time and place of the paternity test. We left Judah's office deflated but anxious about our next steps.

As we entered the car preparing to head to the hospital to see Abraham, my phone began to ring. I looked down and saw Momma Hannah's number. My heart began to do jumping jacks but I told it to quiet down so that I could hear what Momma Hannah had to say. Momma Hannah said that she wanted us to know that Abraham was being released from the hospital and the doctors believed that his prognosis at this time was good. I cried out Hallelujah and started thanking God for his mercy towards me and my family. I told Will the good news and he actually pulled the car over and started pointing his hands up in the sky and saying God, thank you and I remember my promise. I looked at him, what promise is that? Will looked at me and said this one is between me and my God babe. Did he say me and my God? Did I really hear what I think I heard? You know, sometimes when God has answered your prayers, you really can't believe that it is finally happening, and you still question what you are seeing and hearing. I wonder if this is a form of disbelief. We say God answers prayers, but do we really truly believe that he does and can answer us? Why are we so shocked when our prayers are answered? I waited over eleven years for God to answer my prayers. Granted, it surely did not come the way that I expected it to come but nevertheless it finally came. My husband is finally coming to terms with the fact that there is someone bigger and greater than him and His name is God. What a revelation. Not sure when the light bulb went off in his head but I am so glad that it finally did.

Lord, how in the world can I ever thank you for showing yourself strong and mighty in every situation we will ever face. What shall I render to you for all of your benefits towards me? Nothing short of my life. I will forever tell people about your faithfulness, your goodness and your love for mankind. Lord, I love you and I want everyone to know that you deserve all of the glory for all of the things you have done. God, I will spend my life spreading your message and letting people know that you are alive and well. It is not your will that anyone should perish but have everlasting life.

Don't people ever sit back and wonder what is this life all about? There has to be more to life than aspiring to be able to purchase expensive clothes, fancy shoes, nice houses and fabulous cars. Do people ever look at the lives of those who can afford to acquire all of those material things and they are depressed, empty and suicidal. Money isn't everything, for what shall it profit a man to gain the whole world and then lose his very soul. There must be a reason why we are all existing on this Earth. This is not our final resting place, and we are only passing through on our way to our heavenly meeting with our Savior Jesus. Yes, our meeting with the one who made it possible for us to reign with Him after we leave this place called Earth. Lord, thank you for thinking of a way to save us after Adam and Eve sinned and fell from grace. Thank you for not giving up on us but redeeming us from the hands of all of our enemies. I suddenly remembered that Momma Hannah was on the phone. I had zoned out and had no idea what more she said after I heard her say that Abraham was being discharged and Will mentioned his promise to God.

I returned to hear Momma Hannah asking me if I was alright. I said yes Momma. How are you doing? She said that she was elated and quite happy about the turn of events. She said that she was having a praise party with the Holy Spirit as the guest of honor. I said Momma, I hear you and I understand completely. Only you know as a mother how it feels to have prayed for your son's deliverance and to have God answer you in such a mighty way. She said yes, chile, you better know that as soon as that church door open, I will be up in there with the loudest shout and the best praise dance that only King David and I know. Yes, Momma Hannah, you have a right to rejoice and don't let nobody take away that praise of yours. Chile, trust me, no-one will be able to do such a thing.

How is Sugar doing? Sugar is doing good but poor thing is weary and tired. She needs a long vacation on somebody's sandy beach. That is what I am talking about Momma Hannah, we all need to go on that same vacation. How is my son Will? Will is good Momma. I gave him the good news and he started thanking God. Momma Hannah said, he did what, did I hear you right? Yes, you did. Will said stop talking about me like I am not here.

Momma Hannah heard Will's comment and said maybe somebody snatched my son and this person is pretending to be Will. Did you ever think about that, Karma? No, Momma, I never thought about that one. I am pretty sure that this is the man that I married though. Will smiled and Momma Hannah proclaimed a loud Hallelujah, thank you again Jesus! How many surprises can a woman take in one day? Momma said she wanted to scream and tell everyone that their blessing is on the way, just wait until your deliverance comes. God's Word is as good as gold. Good as gold I say, good as gold. Amen. With those words, Momma was gone in the wind and I could hear her yelling Hallelujah as she hung up the phone.

CHAPTER- 17

When I got off the phone, Will was smiling. I asked him what was so engaging. He said I could hear my momma screaming Hallelujah on the phone and I could only guess why. Why may I ask? She is thanking God for renewing my mind and for the rebirth of her son. I am screaming Hallelujah right along with her. God is good. That He is, proclaimed Will, that He is.

We were on our way to pick up Faith when the phone rang again. Will and I both looked at each other and wondered what is it this time, good or bad news. I looked down at the phone and realized that it was my friend Oprah. She said girl, I haven't heard from you in ages. Is this how you do your friends? No girl, you know me better than that, but I have been dealing with some craziness on this side of town. She said I can only imagine. I know that Faith is over at Darlene's house. How about we meet over there for a sit down? Will can take Faith home and we will drop you home later. Sounds like a plan to me.

Will, Oprah wants me to hang out with her and Darlene for a while, do you mind taking Faith home and I will follow you guys in a little while? I could really use some time fellowshipping with the girls. He looked at me and said I hope you don't go spilling all of my business, but women will be women. No problem babe, Faith and I will hang out until you return home.

So, we went to Darlene's house and Will took Faith home and I sat down to talk to my girls. Will gave me that look on his way out like don't go telling all my business, but how could I not share my testimony with my fellow prayer warriors. I started by thanking them for their many prayers and I told them that I have learned that sometimes when God answers your prayers, it might not be in the way that you expected it to come, but nevertheless He answers it in the way that will work for your good. I told them about Abraham's diagnosis and the many days spent at the hospital and how I saw a major transformation in my husband when he thought that he was going to lose his brother.

I told them that in the midst of the storm, God kept reassuring me that everything was going to be alright. Often times in life, we take so many things for granted and then in the twinkling of an eye, one situation can change your whole world. I told them how my husband started to call upon the name Jesus and even made a promise to God regarding what he would do if God healed his brother. I told my girls that we just found out that Abraham was being released from the hospital and that his prognosis looked good.

The girls both jumped up at the same time and started dancing and glorifying God for the healing of Abraham and the transformation of my husband. Oprah said Lord Jesus, we have been praying so long for the positive change in this man and that He would come to know your name and to give His life to you. It has finally happened, and we are shocked, not that we didn't know you would do it, but shocked that you have chosen this time to do it. Lord, we thank you for answering our prayers, Lord we thank you for hearing us and finding the meditation of our hearts acceptable in thy sight. Those girls were having a field day dancing and praising all around the room. I said can you both sit down and let me finish.

Darlene said Oh we are so sorry, go ahead with the story, but thank you Jesus as she waved her hand. They sat down and I told them how Will apologized to me for his behavior and told me how sorry he was for taking me for granted and for being a foolish man. I told them that I was beside myself and couldn't believe that I was hearing those words from out of my husband's mouth.

I told them that I wished I could have taped it so that I could replay the splendid scene over and over and over again. God truly answers prayers. No matter how long it takes, He will answer. If you live a disciplined life and you follow the oracles of God and your heart is right, God will grant you the desires of your heart. Glory!

The girls jumped up again and started praise dancing right there in the middle of the living room, high fiving one another and lifting up the name of Jehovah. They started speaking in tongues and running around the room thanking God for coming through. No wonder some people think Christians act crazy, if somebody had walked into that room at that moment, they would have certainly called 911 to come and strap those girls into the stretcher and take them both to the mental institution. But God takes the foolish things of the world to confuse the wise. Their actions might look foolish to an outsider, but God is just soaking up all of that praise and saying look at my children loving on me. I once had somebody ask me, why would God be interested in people just praising Him all day. Well, as a parent, it always feels good when your children appreciate all that you do for them, it feels good when your child lets everybody know that she or he has a great Father or a great Mother. I imagine it is the same way with

God but when I get to Heaven, I will ask Him that question but for now, praising Him is what I love to do.

I had to force the girls to sit down again and then I told them that on our way home from having such an awesome day, there was a woman standing outside of our house. I told them how Will told me to stay in the car and how he and the lady were arguing outside. I told them how the lady left in a huff and she told him that this was not over. Their mouths were agape, and I could see their disappointment and sadness. It gets worse girls. I told them how Will told me that this lady was someone he was involved with for about a year and he broke it off with her and she refused to accept it. Orpah said my God, when will guys learn that if you keep playing with fire, you will get burned one day. Some women are downright dangerous and not interested in playing fair.

I told my girls how the lady whose name is Caroline, called me up and dropped a bigger bombshell on me by telling me that she was the mother of my husband's son. O my God, both Darlene and Orpah jumped up off the couch and started walking around the room as if they were on street patrol. They walked from one corner of the room to the other side of the room and then they reversed. I knew that they were speechless and unsure of what to say but they were pacing and waiting for guidance from the Holy Spirit.

Darlene said, I really don't know what to say? This is really heavy. How are you doing Karma? I said I am actually doing okay, believe it or not. I told them about my conversation with God and how He gave me reassurance that everything was going to be alright. I told them how God is turning this awful situation around for my good. I told them that I am still taking things one day at a time, but God has given me a peace that I cannot even begin to explain. I wished things were different, but it is how God chose to answer our prayers so if He brought me to it, He will bring me through it.

Told them about what had transpired at the hospital and how we had to go and hire an attorney to deal with Caroline's unwillingness to have Will visit his child outside of her home. They both decided that it was time for all of us to bring this situation to God. We felt empowered since we knew that He had heard our prayers and answered us before. Darlene said, Father Jehovah, you are the all Sufficient One, you are the Alpha, Omega, Beginning and Ending of all things. Before this situation arose, you knew how you would solve it. All three of us stand united in prayer seeking healing for Will's son, and God seeking a softening of Caroline's heart to know that the relationship is over and that she must let go. Father, only you can deal with hearts. Touch her right now in the name of Jesus, and please help ease the pain she must be feeling and deliver her from the soul ties that she has created with someone else's husband. Father, in the name of Jesus, we pray for a speedy resolution of this matter. We touch and agree believing and knowing that it is already done, in Jesus name we pray.

It is funny how people say that they cannot pray, but prayer is simply speaking to God. Some prayers sound so nice and flowery and you just know that God heard them, but God is not interested in the words but the heart behind the prayer. If your heart ain't right, and the prayer is powerful in the ears of the hearers, it means nothing to God. He looks at the heart. You can say eight words, Father in the name of Jesus, save me and God will respond faster to you than someone who is praying with sweet sounding words. It is not about the prayer but the heart. I told the girls that things between Will and I were good except for this situation that we are currently facing. I assured them that I know that God will work it out for us. Oprah and Darlene said that they don't know if they could be as strong as me if they were in a similar situation. I told them that God does not give us more than we are able to bear.

I reminded them of the woman caught in adultery and how the religious people wanted to stone her, but Jesus said that he who is without sin cast the first stone. No-one could throw the first stone since we all have sinned and fallen short of the glory of God. It is up to God and his angels to judge and my job is to live a life well-pleasing to my Master, following his Word to the best of my ability.

They both looked at me and I could see tears in their eyes. Orpah said you deserve so much more, and you don't need to be going through this and I feel so sad. Darlene said I understand where you are coming from and I pray for your strength. I said it is so easy for us to quote scriptures, but God is looking at whether we apply those scriptures when we face difficult situations in life. Will you lay down and wallow in tears or will you rise up and say that I know that my Redeemer lives. Will you trust God to show you the way out of the dark valley or will you do your own thing? I told them that at times, I wanted to just stay mad and angry and live in my pain, but God said how do I get glory out of that pain. I get glory when others know that you are in pain but nevertheless see you marching forward knowing that I will give you the victory in due time. God is busy. He will fix your case in due time and when He fixes it no man can unfix it. I call these the lessons of life. The lessons are learned through walking with God and having a personal relationship with Him. It is so important for us to know God and He wants us to know Him and we know Him through His Word. I told the girls, please continue to praise God with me. Don't stop. We prayed and believed God when things were dire, now things are looking a tad bit better, it's time to pray and praise Him even more.

Girls, I can't lie and say that I am not hurting because I am. Every time that I think about the fact that my husband has a child with someone else, I feel as if someone punched me in my gut. I look at the child, his name is Imani, and I feel the same pain, but he is a child and I can't hold him accountable for what Will and Caroline did. I have to put on my big girl bloomers and deal with the situation like a woman.

Trust me, I am going to be fine and my marriage will survive this attack. We will always face consequences for our actions, whether good or bad. God forgives us when we go against His Word but there are still consequences that follow us. If you are a child of God, He will give you the grace to deal with those consequences. I said, Lord Jesus, grant me the grace to deal with this consequence

HERE. At least it is one consequence, one child, and not consequences, two or more children. Can't say what would happen to Will if I were facing consequences. We all looked at each other and burst out laughing. Yes, it was so good to have this time to talk with my girls, good indeed.

CHAPTER- 18

Let me tell you something, Family Court is no joke. First of all, you are all cramped up in some small courtroom spilling your guts in front of a so-called impartial officer. Why can't folks work out their issues outside of court? Why must we invite another person into the mix to come in and tell us how we are supposed to be doing things? The whole thing is so absurd that it is even comical if it weren't so serious.

We walked into the court room and spotted Caroline right away whispering to her lawyer. Judge Ally McBeale appeared and sat on the bench. She beckoned to her court officer that she was ready, and the roll call began. Thank God we were third on the list. I couldn't bear staying there one minute longer than I needed to be there. It was so sad to see so many families in turmoil and in situations that were way over their head. I wonder how different lives would be if we all just heeded the Word of God especially when it came to sex.

God said sex is for married people and everybody act like they never heard the word fornication. I am not here to judge but clearly if you disobey the command, there will be a price to pay. Nobody ever wants to pay the price, but they always think that they will be able to steal free love on the side. At some point, you will have to pay the piper and when it's time to pay, everybody wants to cry foul and look for ways to escape the bounty on their head. God said don't do it and that's enough for me.

Don't get me wrong. It's not as if I hadn't indulged in sexcapades before marriage, but I always ended up with my heart broken and enough tears to fill a river. It is interesting to see women sit up in church praising God and then go home to shack it up with their man. I am not judging, I'm only saying. Sister, how is that going to work out for you? How do you think that is really going to end up? You have given the Devil free rein to tie you up in knots and knock you down when he thinks that you will not be able to get back up.

Sisters, we have got to do better. As I look around this courthouse, all I see is black and brown faces and little kids hanging on to their mama's skirt tails. One wise man once told me, if you want a man to respect you, then you have to show him that you are respectable. Whether true or not, men feel that if you give them the goodies then you will also give it to the next man. Of course, we know that is nonsense, but that is how men think and nobody is going to debunk them of that thinking, especially me and you.

Ladies, if you want to get married, if the man says he is not ready for marriage, believe him, he is not ready for marriage. Furthermore, he is really not into you and that is okay. If he is too dumb to recognize your shine and your brilliance, hey, he is too dumb for you to want to marry. If you are saved and living for God, let that man know that your goodies belong to your husband and no-one gets to sample the goods without paying the price.

It is so sad to see how many people have been fooled by slippery words and deceitful moves. Even if you are not saved, God's principle remains the same. Keep your legs closed, tell the man no and you will see how fast he will put a ring on it. We must teach our children the right things. Who wants to end up in this dreadful place before Judge McBeale waiting for her to decide who gets to keep the children? It just ain't right and we must do better.

I see both Will and Caroline head to the Judge's bench along with their attorneys. I could see the Judge shaking her head and saying it is unreal that two mature individuals can't come to an agreement regarding visitation of a minor child. Then she smirks and says of course I presumed that I was dealing with mature people, but I guess not. See what I mean. You come into court and give these pompous judges the right to degrade and malign your good name. When will we learn? Before I could finish my thoughts about that Judge McBeale, the matter was postponed for a couple of weeks for Will to take a paternity test. A paternity test? Caroline was furious. Why isn't he just consenting that the child is his? Will was going to consent, but his attorney advised him against it. If Caroline could have kicked Will's attorney's behind and get away with it, she would have done so. Anyway, round 2 will arrive soon enough. I can't wait.

On our way home, we decided to stop by Abraham and Sugar's house to see what they were up and doing. We arrived to see Abraham and Sugar lounging in the back yard. I pulled up a chair and Will sat down next to me. Wow, Abraham exclaimed. It is good to be back in the comfort of my home. Hospitals are not made for men. Nothing but vampires up in there seeking your blood and they are never satisfied. Sugar kissed her husband and said it is certainly good to have him back home. Running back and forth to that hospital has taken its toll on my body, nothing but aches and pains. Abraham said, babe I apologize to you for putting you through all of this. If I had only listened when you were talking to me about my health, I am sure it would not have reached that unfortunate level.

Abraham turned to Will and asked, why are men so hard-headed especially when it comes to our health? Must be a macho thing, we think that we are invincible so no need to listen to a woman and no need to go to see some doctor who is only going to give us bad news. Isn't that true, Will? It certainly is brother, but we have to learn from our mistakes and try not to repeat them. Anyway, what are the doctors saying? Well, I have to keep going in for those vampires to keep checking my blood to make sure that I remain okay. How do you feel? Well, I feel great to tell you the truth. I feel like I am back to my old self but without the pain. Will said, great to hear brother. I thought I was going to lose you and I wasn't prepared for that at all. You forced me to go and seek God and to make amends with the man upstairs. Abraham said what, you did what? Yes man, I have even been going to church with my lady here. It is as if He has given me a second chance and a new lease on life. This God thing is kind of alright.

Abraham walked over to his brother and put his hand on his forehead to check his temperature. Is this really my brother talking? Will said of course it is, I am just a changed man. I am even thinking of getting baptized and giving my life over to God. Lord knows, I have made a mess of things doing it my way. Man, my sickness did all of that for you. Yes man, it did, it made me realize that there is someone greater than me or you. Someone who is controlling the heavens and the Earth and everything in between. I want to know more and more about this God. I have finally found peace with this God. I am not perfect, but I am learning how to perfect some of my ways, and I am learning how to walk uprightly before Him.

Man, I want to invite you to church with me on Sunday. Abraham said I am all in. Sugar and I looked at each other and giggled. Our God was working right before our eyes. Abraham said I was thinking that I needed to go and tell the Man upstairs thank you for saving my life. It was touch and go there for a while, but God has surely been good to me. Will said yes, he has, and we have so much to be grateful for.

Will said, I often wonder why it is so hard for men to come to the Lord and surrender their lives. It might go back to what you were saying before about our health and us being macho and not wanting anybody to tell us what to do. Our churches are filled with women but where are the men? Why is it so hard for men to kneel before their Maker, why are we filled with so much pride? It takes nothing away from us to praise Him and it takes nothing away from us to worship Him. In fact, it takes some of the burden away to give those problems over to someone greater than ourselves.

Abraham agreed and said you sound like a preacher there, my brother. Will said, I know but there is a praise on my inside that I cannot keep to myself. I feel like I want to go on top of buildings and scream about the goodness of Jesus. Wow, when I look at this woman and see how God allowed her to stick with me even with my stupidity, it is enough for me to want to do back flips. It is only by the grace of God why she is still here by my side.

Will told Abraham that I finally came clean and told Karma about Caroline and Imani. Abraham looked at him and then looked at me in shock. Sugar asked Abraham if he was alright. Abraham said that he was, but he wanted to know once again, if Will was feeling okay.

Will said I am feeling great. No more secrets between us man, secrets destroy marriages. Sugar looked at me and I could see that she wanted to ask what was going on, but she kept the question to herself. I suddenly realized that I had not told her about the affair, and I vowed to fill her in later. After kicking it with Abraham and Sugar for a couple of hours, laughing and talking, we decided to call it a day and to head home.

As we were walking to our car, Will got down on his knees and asked me Karma, given all that I have put you through, would you marry me all over again? I pondered his question for a few minutes, and I said Will, let me answer it this way. Given all the stuff that we put Jesus through, do you think he would give His life again for each one of us? He said yes and I looked at him and said that is my answer. God's love is unconditional. I am not comparing myself to Jesus, but I took a vow before God and the angels to love, honor, and respect you all the days of my life. I am striving to display unconditional love even in the midst of every storm that we will ever face. Marriage is not about feelings but about a contract I made with God. I intend on keeping the promise that I made to Him.

I am not interested in just quoting scriptures, but I want to test the Word of God. I want to see all of His promises come through in my life and that of my family and loved ones. I want my life to be a living sacrifice, and after all of this, I want God to say well done Karma, good and faithful servant. When the going got tough, you did not lose faith in Me. When the tides were going against you, you towed the course and waited for my deliverance to come. So yes Will, I would marry you all over again. Through this experience, God has worked on me and showed me how to increase my faith and believe in Him for my miracle. How can I ever repay God for what he has done for us? How could my faith ever be strengthened without this test? I don't get to choose the test, but I get to choose whether I will pass it or not. I believe, by the grace of

God, I have passed this one. Will looked at me and said yes baby, you passed this one with flying colors. Now, let the church say Amen.

CHAPTER- 19

I woke up to Will's snoring, sounding like a roaring lion seeking whom he could devour. Not me buddy, I am getting out of the lion's way. I hopped out of bed and went to sit in the living room chair. I started to read my morning devotion and then I started to pray and have my early morning talk with God. Lord, why you love me so I will never know. I see my wretchedness every day and I am so far away from your righteousness. Help me Father to be all that you would want me to be, help me to worship and love you the way that you desire. Sometimes I feel like my best is not good enough, but Lord I am asking you to help me to make it into your resting place. I want at that appointed time to make it into my heavenly mansion filled with gold. Prepare me Lord for yourself, make my mind right and my heart right. You are the Lord and you never fail. Help me to walk in the narrow way and to live a life that is pleasing to you God. Help me to do your will and not my own. Let others see you in me and want to follow this God that has blessed and kept me. Although I have troubles, although I have pain, help me to look beyond me and surrender my will to yours. Help me to patiently await your answer since you know what is best for me.

As I was sitting there praying and talking to God, a fleeting thought crossed my mind. Why was Caroline so freaked out about the paternity test? Could it be? At that moment, Will came out of the room and I got up to start preparing breakfast. This was his big day, he was going to be baptized today. Faith stumbled out of her room and jumped on Will. Daddy, you are about to play in the church pool today. We both laughed.

Water baptism was an outward manifestation of our faith and an act that God desired for us to do in order to show the world that we are now adopted into His Kingdom and we are one of His children. We are taught that if you believe in your heart and confess with your mouth that God raised Jesus from the dead, then you will be saved. As Faith and Will ate up, I began to marvel at the fact that my husband was going to see the King this morning. I felt like jumping up and down and running around the whole world to let them know that God has answered the many prayers that went up for my husband. God is alive and well. Put your trust in the Lord. He will bring you out. He will win the battle for you. Give Him praises in advance for your victory. Give Him glory! I feel a praise coming on. Lord Jesus, you have done it again. Why do we ever doubt? You always make a way for us, your children. Today, my husband is joining the Army of the Lord. Can't wait to see what great things you are going to do in his life. Before I knew it, both Faith and Will were gone from the dining table and I realized that it was almost time to leave the house. O my, if I keep this up, I might miss the entire baptism.

When we entered the church, Momma Hannah, Abraham, and Sugar were all waiting for us. Oprah and Darlene were sitting up front with their husbands. I hope that that they understood where I was coming from the other day. It is one thing to quote scriptures, but we all get into trouble when it is time to put the Word into practice. Are we living that thing? Are we displaying the fruits of the spirit, love, joy, peace, goodness, meekness, gentleness, long-suffering and self-control? If we as Christians, can't display the traits of the Holy Spirit, even in the worst of circumstances, then who are we preaching to? Who are we going to convert? Change-- let it first start with us. Yes, that person in the mirror.

Anyway, I am so excited about God. I want to brag about Him, I want to boast about my Savior and my King. There is a miracle in this room, and it has my name and my husband's name on it. It has my daughter's name on it. Glory. I am going to put a praise on this one. God has come through in a major way. No matter what came up against this marriage, I have kept my praise, I have kept my joy, and I have kept His peace.

When the praise and worship team started ministering, I found myself at the altar giving God all of the praise and honor for what He had done. When it was baptism time, I couldn't stop weeping. The journey was only beginning with my husband as a saved man, but I am standing here today to bless the Lord for the great transformation. As he went down in the water, Momma Hannah held my hands and held Sugar's hands and lifted them up to the Heavens and said thank you Jesus.

When he came up out of the water, I saw tears streaming down his face. He had finally surrendered his life to the Lord. May God continue to reveal more and more of Himself to Will. May God continue to grant him victory in every battle He will face. The Devil is not after those who don't believe but he is after those who have decided to follow Jesus. May Will overcome every trial, temptation and tribulation the enemy will throw at him. Lord, we put our hope and trust in you. You will never let us down.

I looked over at Abraham and I also saw tears streaming down his face. I knew right then and there that Abraham would soon follow in his brother's footsteps. After the baptism, the Pastor took to the altar and gave us a message about forgiveness. He told us that forgiveness is not about the other person, but it is really about you setting yourself free from that situation.

After the sermon, the Pastor asked for those who wanted to give their lives over to the Lord and just as I suspected, Abraham's hands went up. Momma Hannah, Sugar and I started weeping. I am not sure who cried the longest, but they were tears of joy. What could we render to God for all of His benefits towards us? What a God! When Abraham got back to his seat, Faith turned to him and said, Uncle Abraham, I guess next week you get to play in the church pool too. He said, yes Faith, something like that and we all laughed.

I couldn't have asked for a better ending to a more perfect day.

CHAPTER- 20

And just like that, the next day was a day straight from the pit of hell. How soon the good times were forgotten. It started as always with a phone call. Will's attorney was on the phone and wanted to speak with him right away. He said that Caroline and her attorney had filed papers seeking an Order of Protection against Will. Caroline was claiming that she was fearing for her life and Will had threatened to kill her if she did not allow him to see his child. She was asking for an immediate hearing in Court. The hearing was scheduled for tomorrow. How in the world can this be? When Will got off the phone, I asked when did this incident supposedly occur? He said the attorney told him that the legal papers said that Will paid her a visit on Saturday night. What a big lie! Will and I were together all-day Saturday, he never left the house.

What this woman will not do to bring drama into this household. She keeps letting the Devil use her in ways that she should resist, and he will flee. This is just incredible stuff. Women need to stop. Whenever there is an issue with a man, they always pull this domestic violence card so that the courts will be sympathetic to their imagined fear. I am not saying that there are not men out there who deserve to be jailed for verbally and physically abusing women, but how difficult it becomes to tell the difference between lies and truth. So many women cry foul with their lies of abuse that when a woman really needs help from her abuser, we look at her sideways and in disbelief.

Nowadays, everybody knows that all you have to do and say is domestic violence and courts will rush to judgment since no-one wants to have that one case that makes the news because the judge did not lock up the alleged offender or did not issue that Order of Protection. It is a very serious topic and should not be taken lightly. However, we must also recognize that there are many women who game the system in order to get back at those individuals that they feel have wronged them. Women and men make up lies in order to get the significant other excluded from homes by seeking Orders of protection under false pretenses. That is not right, and we must change the system.

Now this man has to appear in court and answer to bogus charges and hope and pray that the sitting judge can see through this nonsense of a ploy. Why are we always trying to destroy one another? Okay, the relationship did not work. Cry your tears like every other broken-hearted person and get over it already. She had better let us be. Don't let me have to go down on my knees and cry out to God to force her to leave us alone. I am holding my peace and I pray that she does the same. The nerve of her. I need to pray that God would mend her brokenness, but I am not feeling particularly holy at the moment.

Queen Jackie arose. Now we are talking girlfriend, go right over there and get all ghetto on that behind and upside that head. Put that grease on your face, braid up that hair and put on those sneakers, take out those earrings and let us go, you remember how we do it. All of a sudden, I heard the other voice asking me if I prayed about this matter since I heard about it this morning. I said no. The same voice said, why not? I had no answer. It was easier to just get into my feelings. After reflecting, I realized that I did not pray nor did I seek direction from the Lord on how to handle the matter, I just went right into how to take matters into my own hand. I should have learned this lesson by now, taking matters into your own hands never work and only causes greater trouble for you.

Jacqueline Greene

I immediately went into my prayer closet and called upon Jesus to fix this matter. Father, in the name of Jesus, I need your help, Will needs your help. We need you to make all crooked places straight for us and we need you to clear our pathway to peace. We are wrestling with spirits that are trying to destroy us. We ask in the name of Jesus that you will intervene and fight this battle in the courtroom of Heaven. Intercede for my husband and for me right now in the name of Jesus. Let this case be dismissed and give us total victory in the name of Jesus. Amen.

All of a sudden, I felt that undeniable peace overtake me. I am telling you, don't knock it until you try it. Just say Jesus, help me. Prayer changes things. I dare you to reach out to the Father and pray about that situation and watch Him work it out for you. God's love is unconditional, but his blessings are conditional. You have to do this in order to get that. In other words, if you set you love upon Him and follow his commandments, He has no choice but to hear and to answer you. I know He heard my prayer because He in turn gave me an inner peace that no-one in this world could give me. I just have to now sit back and wait for him to give me the victory in the matter at hand.

I looked at my husband after he got off of the telephone and I sat him down. I said babe, how are you feeling? Oh boy, said Queen

Jackie. You are what we call a foo foo girl. The man knocked up some woman, has a child outside of marriage, his baby mama giving you headaches and you calling the man babe and asking him how he is doing? You need to be smashing him upside his head with my pocketbook if I had one. Can you lend me yours so that I can hit him upside his head for you?

I brushed off Queen Jackie's comments and asked my husband about his well-being. Will responded by saying that he was feeling overwhelmed. I told him that at times like these he has to seek direction from God. Will, the Devil will now be on your tail forever until God calls you home. He knows that he has lost your soul, but he will always try to regain it. Don't give him any leeway to come back into your life. Don't mess with him and he will still mess with you but when you keep messing him up, he will mess with you less and less.

Your faith in God will be tested. It is okay to feel overwhelmed and lost during these difficult times. God will bring you through, I promise you. Don't ever give up on God and He will never give up on you. I am so thankful that I believed God enough to wait for him to turn this marriage around. I am so convinced that my God is amazing, awesome and all that plus all that. Will said Karma, I wish my faith was as strong as yours. I wish I had that close relationship you have with God. Will, it did not happen overnight. It came through the testing of my faith and learning who God is and what he likes and what he hates. You will learn too. It is like trial and error. In time, you will know Him like I do. Will, I don't ever want you to think that my walk with God is perfect, in fact, I bother Him way too much with things that I should already know. But He looks beyond my faults and sees my needs. Will, as a new- born babe in the Lord, I am sure that He has so many angels attending to you and making sure that all of your requests are brought to Him immediately. You are so precious in His sight. Continue to trust the process.

One of my favorite scriptures in the Bible is Proverbs, Chapter 3, verses 5 and 6, "Trust in the Lord with all thine heart, acknowledge Him in all thine ways, lean not unto your own understanding and He will direct your paths. Will, trust Him at all times, our God will never disappoint you.

If you ask for something and you don't get it, believe that it would not have been good for you to have received that thing. It might have killed you, led to your destruction or taken you out of the will of God. God is interested in all areas of our lives. It is His desire that we prosper and stay in good health. Satan is always after God's children, but God always has his angels there to protect us.

Let me tell you something that I have never told you before. One evening I was on my way home from church, it was late, after 12 midnight. I got off the bus and was walking home when I noticed this guy following me. All of a sudden, this car appeared with this lady who asked me if I wanted a lift. It could have even been a man who was driving the car. Up to this day, I am not even sure of the gender of the person who gave me a lift to my house. I believe it was my guardian angel. I was right around the corner from my house, so the angel just drove me around the block. I always remember that night whenever I start to doubt whether God is with me. I know without a shadow of doubt that He is with me.

God loves you Will and He will protect you from dangers unawares. Give this situation over to God and watch Him work it all out for you. Will said Wow, you never told me. I know. Sometimes I wonder if it really happened, but I know that it really did. We are going to be alright Will. God did not bring us this far to leave us. He knows that we are seeking to please Him so why would He not work this out in our favor? God loves it when his children trust him and have faith in his ability to deliver them.

We can choose our own path or choose His path. What will it be my husband? Wifey, I already chose my path when I went to play in the church pool. Wifey, Queen Jackie said, I am about to be sick. I firmly said be quiet. What did you say babe? Nothing Will, I was just muttering to myself. Myself is not my name. Enough already. Karma, yes Will? Thank you for introducing me to this God. Yes Will, O taste and see that the Lord is good. He's incredible, isn't He? He surely is, Wifey, He surely is.

Queen countered, there he goes with that Wifey business again, was he calling you wifey when he was engaged in relations with that woman?? I really think I am going to be sick this time. Enough. Alright. Next.

CHAPTER- 21

Forgiveness is great if you are able to achieve it. Not many people can. They say they forgive, but their forgiveness is questionable. I once had somebody say you should forgive, but don't forget. How is that possible? Doesn't forgiveness mean that I have to forget as well? One wise man told me that you forgive by freeing yourself and the other person, but you don't have to forget the incident. Use the incident as a teaching moment and be careful not to willingly repeat your mistake, if any. The Bible teaches us to forgive as many times as your brother or sister asks you if you want the same forgiveness from your heavenly father in return. We all want God's forgiveness but when it is our time to forgive others, there goes the problem. O help me God.

As we walked into the court room and I see Caroline, I must confess forgiveness is far from my mind. She is sitting there acting as if she is the victimized one in this entire matter. How is she the victim? I am the victim and so is Imani. We did not ask for any of this, but we are right here smack in the middle and thick of the business. What is she up to? What could she possibly hope to get out of this carcass she has created?

Both lawyers were conversing with one another and trying to come to some meeting of the minds. I can't help but to feel sorry for Caroline. Here goes this stupidness in my head again according to Queen. Why should you feel sorry for somebody who is trying to destroy you? Have you no sense, Karma girl? It is kill or be killed. It is fight or die? Do you not see the kind of world we are living in? Why do you insist on living in this fantasy world where people are good, nice and Christianly? The darn Christians are not even Christianly. Listen up Queen, you cannot say that about every Christian. We have to stop looking at others and work out our own salvation. It is so easy to look and see what others are not doing but we never see what we are doing wrong. Are you talking about me Karma, because you know I don't play. No, I agree with you Queen Jackie, the people in this world are out of this world. Karma, sorry to break it to you, but I don't think we are speaking the same language, or you are getting my drift. Stop ascribing positive thinking to somebody who hates your guts. Queen, I can't do that tit for tat business. I am way beyond that nonsense. My hope is that even Caroline will turn around and see the God in me and want to know more about Him. Queen said, Girl, if you don't stop, I will have to find a way to put you in the insane asylum. But Queen, wouldn't you also be putting yourself in there. Yes, and that is the reason why I am trying so hard to get you to think right. I don't want to go into nobody's asylum, but I just may.

Queen, if we don't show God's love to others, then who will? I don't know girl, but it doesn't have to be you. God has enough angels around the Earth to handle His business. We are His angels here on Earth. Karma, I need to rest my head from all of this foolishness. Could you do us both a favor and not have any more thoughts for the day? It is really too much for me to handle today. Of all the people to have in my head, God gives me a comedian.

I bring my mind back to the court room and I see that the Judge has called all sides up to the bench. I hear Will say not guilty and I hear the Judge give a date for the parties to return to court. I hear Caroline's lawyer ask a question about the other proceeding involving child support and visitation. I hear the Judge say this ruling has zero bearing on that case and everyone must comply with all prior orders including the taking of the paternity test. Oh gosh, I almost forgot that Will had an appointment to go and take the paternity test tomorrow morning at 9. I can't wait for all of this to be over and we can move on with our lives. I can only imagine how Will feels. I know he must feel terrible. No roll in the hay could ever be worth all of this trouble.

God gives us commandments and principles to live by in order for us to avoid the pitfalls of life. His desire is for His children to prosper in all areas of their lives. When we disobey, we find ourselves in a whole heap of trouble. Lord, help us to obey your commands.

On the way out of the court room, Caroline rolled her eyes at me and sucked her teeth as if I did something to her. Imagine, you slept with my husband and you have the nerve to be mad with me. How ludicrous is that? This world is upside down. When people are wrong, they want to call it right and what is right, they want to call it wrong. Without the Word of God to guide us, we would all be lost in this madness. Thank God I have morals and I know that messing with other people's husbands is wrong in the sight of God and it displeases him greatly. That girl needs to repent and ask for God's forgiveness instead of getting mad at me for being in my rightful position.

Yes, yes, nobody is perfect. I can see how one can get caught up in adultery especially if the man lies about his marital status, and then you find out he's married after your emotions are all invested in that cheater. You are already in love at that point or you've built ties with him that are not easily broken. I think things get really complicated in any relationship once sex enters the picture. Again, if we followed the way of God and abstained before marriage, we would all save ourselves a whole lot of heartache and headache.

Don't get me wrong, marriage too has its bumps along the road, but God sanctions this relationship above the others. It really shouldn't be about our will but about the will of God. Unfortunately, people don't see it this way anymore. In the last days, people will be lovers of themselves and not lovers of God. Why do we love sin more than obedience and the Word of God? Why do we think that it is more satisfying to plot revenge rather than leaving things in God's capable hands for him to exact revenge on our behalf? Vengeance is mine saith the Lord, but we can't wait on God. In fact, I believe that we think that we can do it better than God can. Wrong. So, Miss Caroline, I will leave you at the cross and in the hands of my God for I have learned that he will deal with you much better than I ever can. Bye Felicia girl, I mean Caroline. See you on the next court date.

CHAPTER- 22

Will and I almost missed the appointment. We both woke up late and immediately started scrambling to make it to the lab on time. We got there just in the nick of time. Once we walked into the laboratory office, no surprise, who do we find sitting up in there? It was raining men. Nothing but men sitting up in that crowded waiting room. Lord, help us to get our lives together so that we can avoid placing ourselves in places like this one. We place ourselves there when we refuse to follow God's principles. God's way is the only way.

God's way includes waiting and having no sex before marriage. I hear women and men saying that they are not committing to marriage without sampling the goods beforehand. Your faith is tested in the waiting. You just have to trust God. I think of it this way. You can sample things beforehand and the sex is slaying, but then you marry, and then it stinks. You ask what happened? Only God knows but wouldn't you have felt better if you had just waited, obeyed and trusted God for that amazing sexual experience after marriage.

I also tell the young girls and young boys not to marry anyone who is not a believer in Christ. When I say believer, this person must demonstrate this belief through water baptism and living a life pleasing to God. You should observe actions, you should study them, love is not an overnight thing. I wish I had known these nuggets of life before I got married. I am not saying that I would not have married Will since we all know that I would have but only when he had given his life over to the Lord. Our waiting would have made my marriage less painful in my estimation.

We waited about two hours before Will was finally called in to take the test. The technician said that the results would be sent directly to the courthouse and we would also receive a copy in the mail after the court date. We left the office and went out for a late breakfast. It was good to be able to have a civil conversation with my husband. Will told me that he often was rude to me because he had so much guilt inside over the things he was doing and the life that he was living. He said that it was as if he were on drugs and didn't know how to stop.

He is thanking God for taking away those sinful desires and temptations. He believes that there is no way that he could have kicked those habits on his own. He wishes that he could tell other men that it is okay to surrender their lives to God. There is nothing weak about knowing that there is a greater power than you. Nothing wrong with living a principled and a purpose driven life. Will wishes that he could have come to this revelation when he was younger. O how his life would have turned out so differently.

In life, we all wish that we could go back and change some stupid things we did in the past, but only God gives us those second chances. Our goal is not to repeat the stupidity but to learn from our mistakes. Will said that he wishes he could tell men in particular that God can change their lives for the better. I know what you mean Will, maybe then those laboratory rooms will empty out. We have got to keep hope alive.

The next day I stopped by Abraham and Sugar's house. I had promised to fill her in, but I just never got the chance before today. Thankfully, Abraham was out and would be gone for a few hours. We sat down and Sugar confessed that she had forced Abraham to tell her what we were all talking about the other day. She wanted to call me but figured she would wait until I felt like sharing. She asked me how I was really doing? I told her that I was coming along and each day things were getting a little easier.

I told her that it was only by the grace of God and He was keeping me. I explained to her Caroline's antics as well as her anger towards Will and me. I told her that I go back and forth between my anger towards Caroline and compassion for her soul. Sugar told me that she understood exactly what I was going through.

She told me that a few years back, she caught Abraham cheating on her. She said that she was so ashamed and embarrassed that she didn't tell one soul and even pretended that it was not happening. She said that she had to delve deep inside her soul to seek God and ask for direction. She told me that if she had told people about his infidelity, she is sure they would have told her to leave him. Sugar said in moments like those, you don't need to take your business to Tom, Dick and Harry or Tina, Debbie and Hilary, but you need to seek God. She described a similar experience to mine except there was no child involved that she knows of anyway. Sugar told me that it is possible to rebuild the trust in the marriage after a period of time.

In the beginning, she said that she always wanted to follow him to see where he was going. In fact, I did follow him a couple of times, but it only made me weary and angry. One day I just cried and cried and poured out my heart to God. I had to ask God to repair my marriage and to help me in my brokenness. It wasn't an overnight process, but time healed those wounds.

We both concluded that oftentimes women feel as if they did something wrong. The real truth of the matter is that whatever the reason for the cheating, it had nothing to do with the woman but everything to do with the selfishness of the man. Sugar said that she used to wonder about the love a person has for their mate if they indulge in cheating. I told her that I used to ask that question too, but I concluded that if he does love me, he needs to love me more. She agreed. She said that she and Abraham are in a better place now, but it wasn't easy. She told me not to give up on Will, but to continue to trust God. After all, you waited eleven years for God to answer you and now that He has, it would a shame to give it all up since His answer came with some challenges.

Sugar and I talked about our faith in God and how it must appear foolish to others. Foolish indeed said my Queen. Sugar talked about how her faith in God has also deepened since Abraham gave his life to the Lord. Things have only improved in my marriage. I feel like I can counsel other couples who are going through this struggle. Sugar told me to hang in there and the pain will continue to lessen as the days go by. It was good to hear Sugar's testimony. If God did it for her, I am confident that I am on the right track and he will do it for me. Thank you, God, for leading me here today. I really needed to hear Sugar's words of encouragement.

CHAPTER- 23

Today we are heading into Family Court to deal with the visitation issue. Hopefully, we will leave the courthouse today with a visitation schedule that we can all manage. As we enter the court room, Judge McBeale is already on the bench. She calls our case immediately and Will, Caroline and their respective lawyers approach the bench. Judge McBeale opened up the file and asked whether both parties had reached an agreement regarding visitation with the minor child.

Caroline's lawyer said that his client was consenting to the father's visitation with the child, but she was objecting to visitation at any place other than at her house. Judge McBeale asked why was Caroline imposing such limitations on where the visits were to take place? Instead of waiting for her lawyer to answer, Caroline said that she refused to have any other woman around her young child. The Judge told Caroline that her rationale was unacceptable, and absent a justifiable reason, she was not going to limit visitation only to her house. She told Caroline that she can return to court to seek supervised visitation if something in the future warrants such supervision. The Judge started to inquire as to their respective visitation schedules when she stopped and said that she was putting the cart before the horse.

She opened an envelope in the file and stared at it for a minute and then said hold on, we have a problem here. This report says that the likelihood of paternity is zero percent. Will looked at Caroline and shook his head and Caroline said there must be some mistake. The Judge said no mistake here. The report is quite clear. The probability of paternity for this gentleman is zero percent.

Then the Judge lit into Caroline. She said I am so sick and tired of women using our courtrooms as some sort of game show entitled "Guess Who My Baby Daddy Is. This is ridiculous. It is one thing to come in here saying that you are unsure who the father of your child is, things happen, but women come in here demanding this and demanding that knowing darn well that the possibility exists that they have the wrong man in the court room. They continue to play these games until their lies are discovered and frankly, it makes us women look low and foolish.

It is one thing to come to court humbly and ask us to help you find the right man, but you come here demanding that the child not visit at the man's house because his wife will be around. Guess what, news flash, his wife was always around. Then she turned to Will and told him that he dodged a bullet and he needs to mend his wicked ways.

The Judge started screaming at Caroline stating how she wasted her time, wasted the court officer's time, the stenographer's time, the clerk's time and everybody's time. She told Caroline that she needs to find her child's father and not to wait until the child is 18 to start looking for him. It is unfair to the child.

Have you ever seen that show Paternity Court? It is disgraceful to see how many women don't know who their child's father is. Young lady, I am not trying to be mean to you, but you have to think about the best interest of your child. As difficult as this may be, you have to face it and make it right for your child. Now, this child has bonded with this man for over a year and he's not the father. How is that fair to your young son? What is this man supposed to do with this emotional attachment he now has with this child and how is the child going to feel when this man exits his life? Get it together for the sake of your child. And one last piece of advice, they might counsel me for this, but I am going to say it anyway, my mother used to tell me, and I am telling you, leave people's husbands alone. And one more thing, as my auntie Madea would say, close your legs to married men. And with that, this matter is adjourned.

Oh my God! I couldn't have told Caroline off any better than Judge McBeale. She let her have it in a good and professional way. Wow. You never know how or when Karma will clap back. Can't nobody fix a situation like God. Will is not the father. Oh my God! Can somebody pinch me, is this really true? Did this really just happen?

I looked over at Will and he looked shocked and angry. He turned to Caroline and said I am so glad that God brought me back to my senses before I got more involved with you and your lying behind. She turned to him and said I guess we are all even, every cheater deserves a cheater. He just shook his head and said I will pray for you. She said all of a sudden you want to pray for me, you found religion, good luck with that one. She looked at me and said I told you that you picked a real winner. I refused to be a partaker in other people's sins, so I decided to keep quiet. She just shook her head and walked away. I felt relieved. God came through for us—again. Father, how many ways is there to say thank you? Help me to find one that will truly be pleasing to you.

You deserve all of the glory and praise for working this one out in a way that I never imagined.

I am not sure how many people will emerge with my testimony but if you find yourself in my situation, and your husband's paternity test comes back positive, continue to trust God. I was prepared to trust God even if I had to walk the path filled with baby mamma drama. Thanks be to God that I don't have to walk that path. But the most important point is that I was prepared to do so.

Now listen to me, I am not advocating for anyone to stay in an abusive relationship, but I am saying that God is able to fix that marriage. He is able to repair what others would call the unrepairable. Whether you stay or leave your marriage is personal and only you should make that decision. Just remember that there is no situation that our God cannot handle.

Marriages are hard work and many people enter into them thinking that they have found love on Easy Street. Oh, he said he loves me, and I love him, so all will be well. Now wait a minute there, not so quick, let me tell you something that I have learned through my experience. Marriage is not so much about love or feelings, but it is more about a promise you made to God. If you're going to renege on that promise, involve God in the decision-making process since marriage is a mystery and only God can decode it.

What will make you break that contract with God? Will infidelity, bad attitude, abuse, nasty hygiene, anger, gossip, the list can continue forever. We all have different answers to those questions but in the midst of our funk and fight, do we trust God to make it better? Again, I am not advocating for anyone to stay in an abusive relationship, so please don't start with the hate mail. If your man is abusing you, and you choose to remain in your marriage, it may be wise for you to separate while you wait for God to do His thing. I am not advocating for you to remain with that man if your life is in danger. Clearly, that is a choice you will have to make. Again, my point is that God can fix any situation.

Will interrupted my thoughts by walking over to me and lifting me out of my seat and kissing my hand. Queen Jackie said I don't know what's worse, those thoughts you were just having or that kiss on the hand. Disgusting. I shrugged her off to hear Will say thank you babe for sticking with me and for believing in this marriage even when I was at my worse.

He threw a kiss up to Father God and said thank you again Sir. I could almost hear God say, you are welcome son. Well, well, you ask, where do we go from here, not sure, but I am glad to say that wherever it is, we will go there together. Stay blessed. Peace out. Love from your girl Karma. Remember Karma will always clap back.

www.ingramcontent.com/pod-product-compliance
Lightning Source LLC
Chambersburg PA
CBHW060436130626
46555CB00005B/2386